D0291573

Mary-Kate and Ashley
Sweet 16

#1: Never Been Kissed
#2: Wishes and Dreams
#3: The Perfect Summer
#4: Getting There
#5: Starring You and Me
#6: My Best Friend's Boyfriend
#7: Playing Games
#8: Cross Our Hearts
#9: All That Glitters
#10: Keeping Secrets
#11: Little White Lies
#12: Dream Holiday
#13: Love and Kisses
#14: Spring into Style

Coming soon:
#16: Truth or Dare

California Dreams

By Kimberly Morris

HarperEntertainment
An Imprint of HarperCollins*Publishers*

A PARACHUTE PRESS BOOK

A PARACHUTE PRESS BOOK

Parachute Publishing, L.L.C.
156 Fifth Avenue, Suite 302
New York, NY 10010

Published by
📖 HarperEntertainment
An Imprint of HarperCollins*Publishers*
10 East 53rd Street, New York, NY 10022-5299

SWEET 16 books are created and produced by Parachute Publishing, L.L.C., in
cooperation with Dualstar Publications, a division of Dualstar Entertainment
Group, LLC., published by HarperEntertainment, an imprint of HarperCollins
Publishers.

ISBN 0-06-059522-1

HarperCollins®, 📖®, and HarperEntertainment™ are trademarks of HarperCollins
Publishers Inc.

First printing: June 2004

Printed in the United States of America

Visit HarperEntertainment on the World Wide Web at
www.harpercollins.com

10 9 8 7 6 5 4 3 2 1

chapter one

"**Y**ou sure drink a lot of coffee!" The cute customer sitting at the coffee bar made a silly "concerned" face.

I laughed, but I was really embarrassed. It wasn't even 9:00 A.M. yet, and this was my third trip to the Ooh La Latte Café. The guy probably thought I kept coming back so I could talk to him. He'd flirted with me the first two times I was in here. Nothing icky. Just silly stuff like telling me coffee could stunt my growth.

I pushed my blond hair back over my shoulders. "It's not for me."

"Uh-oh! That sounds like denial. How are you going to beat this coffee habit if you don't admit you have a problem?"

"It's for clients," I explained. "I ordered their lattes with whole milk. But they wanted two percent milk. So I came back. *Then* they decided they liked plain coffee better than hazelnut. So here I am again."

My purple cell phone rang. I dug it out of my *Weddings by Ava* tote bag. "Hello?"

"Ashley, Carly would like a pastry. Pineapple. But only if it's fresh." It was Ava, my boss and the top wedding planner in Beverly Hills.

"I'm on it." I hoped the pastries here were up to Carly's standards. It would really be embarrassing to come back *again*. "Does Nathan want one, too?"

I held on while Ava asked Nathan. She was back in two seconds. "He says yes. Any kind is fine with him."

Typical. Carly is very demanding. Her fiancé, Nathan, is really laid back. Not the kind to make a fuss about coffee or anything else. But Nathan is also way nuts about Carly. So whatever it takes to make her happy, he goes along with.

"I'll be back in five minutes," I promised Ava, clicking off. I placed the coffee and pastry order with the girl working behind the counter and waited for the next round of teasing from the cute guy.

He rubbed his chin. "If I were a detective, I would say that you're buying coffee for someone famous . . . maybe even Nathan Richie and Carly O'Connor, aka 'The Wedding of the Year.'"

My mouth fell open. "How did you know that?"

He tapped his right temple. "I'm psychic."

I rolled my eyes.

"Okay. Okay. I saw Nathan Richie and Carly O'Connor pull up and park in front of that house down the street that says *Weddings by Ava*. You can't miss them in that Jag convertible. Your tote bag says *Weddings by Ava*. So I put all the clues together and deduced that . . . *you* are Ava."

That made me laugh. My sister, Mary-Kate, and I just turned sixteen. That would make me a little young to be one of the top wedding planners in the business.

"Close but no. I'm not Ava. I'm just Ava's lowly summer assistant, Ashley."

He shook my hand. "I'm Greg Johnson, also a lowly summer assistant. I'm working at my dad's law office down the street. Any chance of coming to your office and snagging an autograph?"

I shook my head. "If you've read anything about this wedding, you know it's top secret. Nobody's allowed into the office. Even the delivery people have to leave stuff outside the door. You never know who might be a spy for one of the newspapers."

"I guess the reporters can get pretty aggressive, huh?"

That was a total understatement. Reporters

had been calling and hanging around Ava's ever since Carly and Nathan's engagement was announced. They were dying for details about the wedding. It was going to be an old-fashioned, over-the-top Hollywood extravaganza, and Carly wanted everything top secret until the big day.

"Would you believe that some reporters have offered me bribes for information? Money. Concert tickets. You name it."

He nodded. "Sure. I'd believe it. Carly O'Connor and Nathan Richie are the ultimate glam couple. They're both movie stars. She's gorgeous. He's handsome. And they're both young. Who wouldn't be interested?"

Even though Ava is one of the hippest and most popular wedding planners in Los Angeles, and she has lots of celebrity clients, getting hired to plan Carly and Nathan's wedding was a huge deal. I think everyone assumed Carly would pick some big New York City planner, someone who had worked with "society" people or European royalty or something. According to several celebrity sites on the Internet, Carly had surprised everyone: Her first choice was Weddings by Ava in Beverly Hills.

Ava's permanent assistant, Jenna, was having a baby this summer. I had helped Ava out with my cousin, Jeanine's, wedding a few months earlier, so

Ava hired me to fill in for Jenna for the summer.

But Carly was so demanding, she was turning into a full-time job herself.

My phone rang again. "Hello?"

"Carly is waiting for her pastry," Ava reminded me. "She says she feels her blood sugar dropping." Ava's voice sounded a little tight. I could tell she was getting rattled.

Carly does this thing where she taps her foot and keeps checking her watch. That's to let everybody know she's not happy. It can be very unnerving.

"I'll be right there!" I waved at the girl behind the counter. She nodded to let me know she was finishing up the order.

I started feeling pretty rattled myself. I wanted to do everything just right. When I'd worked for Ava before, I wound up getting fired, basically for not following instructions or acting fast enough. I eventually fixed the problem and managed to impress Ava enough for her to hire me again when she needed help. But no way did I want to get canned a second time.

It was humiliating enough being fired once. If I got fired from the same job twice, I'd never be able to hold my head up again.

The coffee girl handed me the bag. I waved at Greg. "Gotta go. The clients are waiting. Good luck at the law firm."

He waved. "Good luck with your coffee habit."

I made a face at him and opened the door. But I didn't make it all the way out. My tote bag caught on the door handle.

"Here." Greg came over and opened the door so I could escape.

"Thanks," I said.

"Will you be back here tomorrow?" he asked.

"I may be back here in ten minutes," I answered. We both laughed.

"I'll be here for sure," he said. "This is my regular stop before work. So I hope I'll get to see you again tomorrow."

He waved, and I hurried away. I was flattered but also a little torn. Greg Johnson was cute. And he was obviously interested in me. But I had a boyfriend. A major, serious boyfriend named Aaron who was seriously nice and seriously cute, with dark hair and the bluest eyes.

Aaron was down in the dumps these days because he still hadn't found a summer job. As I headed up the street, I made a mental note to call him that afternoon as soon as I could take a break.

Ava's business was booming, so she'd recently left her small third-floor rented office for a large five-room cottage. The cottage was on a fancy street filled with quaint old restored houses that had been turned into law offices, ad agencies, architecture firms, and clothing and gift boutiques.

Weddings by Ava was in a cream-colored building with pink-and-white trim. It looked like a wedding cake, I thought. I hurried past all the charming houses, eager to get back to work. But when Weddings by Ava came into view, my heart sank.

Oh, no!

A huge mob of reporters was gathered out in front. Photographers swarmed around Nathan's car, cameras flashing.

I'd never get through that crowd. At least not without spilling the coffee and getting the pastry— or myself—soggy.

On the scale of things that can go wrong in a person's life, I know soggy pastry doesn't count for much. But if you knew Carly O'Connor, you'd understand why I was sweating.

I was standing in front of Jilly's, one of the most exclusive gift shops in town—and only two doors down from Ava's.

"Pssst!" The front door of Jilly's opened. A young woman stepped out and beckoned me over with a big smile. "You work for Ava, don't you?"

I'd been in the shop a couple of times, but I didn't recognize this lady.

I nodded. "Yes. I'm Ashley Olsen."

"I'm Tina Landry. Listen, Ashley, I'm new, and I'm a little confused. Could you come inside and tell me what silverware Carly is buying? I know she's one of your most important clients, and I don't want to make any mistakes."

"She's not buying her silver from you. She's getting it from—"

I saw Tina's eyes gleam. "Yes?"

I caught myself. Carly *was* registered at Jilly's. But *not* under her own name. Not even the *owner* of Jilly's knew that Carly was buying from there. Furthermore, Carly was only registered for some pottery pieces. Her dishes were coming from France, and her silver was coming from Italy.

This woman was trying to trick me into giving her information about Carly's wedding plans! She wasn't a saleswoman. She was a *reporter*!

"Sorry," I said, turning away from the woman. "I don't know what you're talking about."

I continued down the sidewalk feeling totally proud of myself. Professional snoops were extremely clever. I had to be careful. I'd just come very close to divulging top-secret information, but I'd seen the trap and sidestepped it. Yea, me!

My phone rang. I grabbed it out of my bag. "I'm coming. I'm coming," I said. "I've just got to figure out how to make it through the mob outside."

"Ashley?"

It wasn't Ava. It was Aaron. Suddenly the day didn't seem like such a disaster.

"I can't talk now. I'm about to charge through a mob of reporters. If you don't hear from me, send help," I said.

Aaron laughed. "Well, at least that sounds more interesting than watching talk shows on TV. Have you ever seen *Gabbing with Gilda*?"

"Uh, no . . ." I eyed the crowd. A few reporters had spotted me approaching. They were murmuring to one another, obviously wondering if I had any connection to Weddings by Ava. I should have ditched the tote bag. But it was so cool. . . .

"Here's how the show works," Aaron went on. "Gilda invites people to come on and talk about their problems, and then—"

The reporters seemed to reach a decision. They charged.

I felt like a kitten facing a herd of wildebeests. "Gotta go!" I threw the phone into my bag, clutched the coffee and pastries to my chest, and lowered my head, preparing for battle.

Everybody was shouting at once.

"Can you tell us the wedding date?"

"Where will the ceremony be held?"

"Is it true that Carly is going to wear a martial-arts wedding dress?"

Just as they closed around me, the front door of Ava's opened. Nathan stepped out onto the sidewalk and let out a loud whistle.

Immediately the mob of reporters turned and raced back in his direction, shouting questions.

He grinned his trademark grin and held up a hand. "Come on, folks. Forget the wedding. Let's talk movies. You heard it here first. Carly and I have signed a deal to do a big-budget action picture together."

"Historical or contemporary?"

"Who's directing?"

"Who's producing and what's the budget?"

I skirted behind the crowd and slipped into the office with coffee and pastry intact. "Saved by Nathan Richie!" I announced.

Ava looked relieved, but Carly O'Connor just laughed. "In the movies Nathan usually saves people by vaulting off the top of a speeding train or something like that. Not by distracting a pack of hungry reporters."

"I'm just happy to be rescued. Here you go." I gave Carly her coffee, then went into the kitchenette to transfer the pastries to a small plate with a lace napkin. Ava was big on what she called "presentation."

I watched Carly out of the corner of my eye. She took a tentative sip, as if she wanted to make sure it was exactly what she'd ordered. Then she took a larger sip and smiled.

"Out*standing*, Ashley. Excellent work. And you did a great job of outrunning the enemy."

I fought the urge to salute. She made me feel as if I'd just saved the world from an alien invasion instead of delivering her coffee. Because of all her acting experience, Carly was almost always "in character," even if the cameras weren't rolling. Right now she was so into learning her new military commando role that even I felt I was playing a part in her action film.

I already knew about the movie Nathan was announcing to the reporters. It was a military action-adventure thriller. Carly was going to play one of the president's Army advisers who winds up back in action to fight a terrorist threat. Nathan was going to play the special missions expert. It was the kind of movie I knew Aaron would love, and we would see it together when it opened.

The front door opened, and in came Nathan. He grinned at me. "Sorry you got trapped out there. I should have known the car would draw reporters. Next time I'll drive my Chevy. They'll clear off now that they've got some pictures and quotes."

"What a bunch of pests," Carly said.

He put an arm around her and kissed the top

of her head. "Come on, babe. Those guys are our best friends," he reminded her. "They're the people who make us stars. This was a great chance to start the buzz about our new picture."

As I watched them together, I realized that Greg Johnson was right. It was hard not to be fascinated by Nathan and Carly. They were such an amazing couple. He was as handsome in person as he was on the screen, and Carly was gorgeous. She was tall, very curvy, and athletic. Her dark hair hung like a shiny curtain down to the middle of her back. I had been practically speechless when I first met them. But now that I knew them a bit more—and how high-maintenance Carly could be—I wasn't so starstruck around them.

My cell rang. It was Aaron. "Hey! What happened to you?" He sounded annoyed.

I took the phone back into the kitchenette. "Uh, sorry. I had a situation. Listen, I really can't talk now."

"Then how about we talk tonight? I'll pick you up around seven. We can hang."

I loved being with Aaron, but he wasn't much of a planner. I'd learned that "hanging" often meant just driving around. I had a long list of errands to run for Ava that afternoon. That would be enough driving around. "I'd rather do something specific," I said.

Aaron sighed. "Okay. How about we go to dinner at the new café on the beach?"

"Sounds great," I said happily. "See you at seven."

I went back into the main part of the office. Carly and Nathan were looking at sketches. Carly put on her glasses and examined each and every detail. "What about the horses?"

"I found them," Ava said proudly. "Twenty perfectly matched white horses trained to pull ten matching carriages."

Ava looks a lot like a movie star herself. She's tall and willowy with platinum hair cut in a bob. And she *always* wears black. Very chic.

Carly shook her head. "Twenty horses and ten carriages won't be enough. I added another bridesmaid. Gina Gupta, the star of *Living Life*."

Wow! I was really blown away. Carly's bridesmaid list already looked like the red carpet at a big premiere. Gina was the hottest new star on TV.

"So we'll need two more horses and another carriage," Carly finished.

I saw Ava's shoulders sag a little. I knew it had taken her about thirty phone calls and two days to find the horses and carriages. Finding more that matched wasn't going to be easy.

Carly reached for a pastry, and I saw her engagement ring glitter. It was a huge square-cut

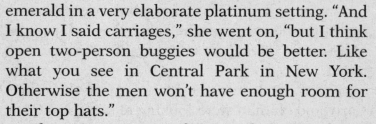

emerald in a very elaborate platinum setting. "And I know I said carriages," she went on, "but I think open two-person buggies would be better. Like what you see in Central Park in New York. Otherwise the men won't have enough room for their top hats."

That got a response from Nathan. "Top hat! I don't have to wear a top hat, do I?"

Carly turned and gave him her 175-watt movie-star smile. I could see Nathan melt. "You will look wonderful in a top hat." She kissed him quickly. "So stop complaining, okay?"

No doubt about it. Carly was a diva, but she had charisma that didn't stop. She'd made our lives pretty miserable with her demands and her whims, but somehow, when she gave you that smile, you stopped being mad about it.

Besides, this wedding was going to put Weddings by Ava on the map. The budget was bigger than that of most movies. Every major Hollywood star would either be in it or at it. I couldn't wait!

Nathan grinned. "Okay. Okay. Whatever. Do I get to pull a rabbit out of it?"

"I'll think about it," Carly promised with a twinkle in her eye.

Nathan's cell phone rang. He stepped over to the window to answer it. He talked in a low tone. I noticed his smile fade a little. He looked at Carly, then pulled the shades aside and looked out at the reporters.

His relaxed face turned tense. Something was clearly bothering him. He said something curt into the phone before putting it back into his pocket.

Usually when Nathan looked at Carly, his expression softened. But this time his face tightened, and he bit the corner of his lip.

Suddenly I remembered something I overheard Nathan quietly ask Ava the other day about refunds for some of the wedding arrangements. Remembering Nathan's question and seeing the look on his face now made me start thinking. . . .

Uh-oh!

Something bad had just happened. And it looked as if it had something to do with their relationship.

I got a worried feeling. If anything happened to ruin this wedding, Ava would be crushed.

And I would be out of a job. Again.

chapter two

"Mary-Kate Olsen, you are a *winner,*" joked Tanya as she piled up goodies on her desk.

"All that stuff is for me?" I asked. I couldn't believe it. As if working with hunky guys at one of the hottest beach clubs in town wasn't enough. Now here was Tanya, the Malibu Beach Club manager, loading me up with totally fabulous free stuff. And I'd only been on the job ten minutes.

It was better than Christmas!

"Here! Put your things in this." Tanya handed me a deep-red microfiber tote with *Mary-Kate* embroidered on one side and *Malibu's Best* embroidered on the other.

The tote was huge—big enough to hold my very own deep-red plush towels, matching robe, and two deep-red tanks that looked as if they'd come right off a fashion runway. Every single thing had the Malibu Beach Club monogram and my initials.

"I feel more like a guest than an employee." I sighed.

Tanya grinned. "You won't once you start working. It's a tough job. But lifeguards are special people, and we try to treat them that way. Come on. I'll take you to the employees' locker room."

I picked up my fabulous red tote and followed Tanya out of the office and down a long hallway. One side of the corridor was a glass wall overlooking the pool area and nearby tennis courts. I could see lots of club employees setting up.

The club had long boards, short boards, and boogie boards on hand for the members. I watched the surf instructors in their board shorts stack the boards on their heads and carry them out toward the beach.

The dining area was at the far end of the club. Delicious buffet lunches were served every day.

No doubt about it, this was a posh club. Pool, beach, tennis courts, golf. And shops, activities, parties, and great food. I was getting psyched. It looked as if the next best thing to being a member was being an employee.

The wall on the other side was covered with photos of little kids. And they all seemed to be smiling right at me.

I got a lump in my throat looking at those

faces. I already knew who they were before Tanya told me. "Every one of those kids was saved from drowning at this very beach club," she said. "If you ever forget why you're here, come take a look at this wall. You'll remember."

It was a good reminder since I'd basically given up a total dream job at *Girlz* magazine to spend the summer working as a lifeguard.

At first my parents thought I was nuts. In a way they were right. *Intern at cool national magazine* looks way more impressive on a college application than *lifeguard*.

But when I looked at those faces . . . Wow! If I had any second thoughts about my job change, they were gone now. What could be more important than saving lives?

"Here's the locker room," Tanya said. "Get changed and then meet Don and the other lifeguards by the pool. I'm going to see the food manager now. Good luck out there."

Tanya left, and I ducked into the locker room to do the quick-change thing. I couldn't wait to get started. Don was the head lifeguard. Not only was he a total hunk, he was a professional swimmer. He was headed for the next Olympics.

There was another girl in the locker room. "Hi!" She gave me a friendly smile. "New?"

"Yes. And totally awed. I'm Mary-Kate Olsen."

"I'm Kelly Mason. I worked here last year. It's a terrific job." We chatted while we changed, and I could tell we were going to get along great. A few minutes later I was ready. Kelly was still braiding her long hair, so I said I'd wait for her in the hall.

I went back out into the hallway all decked out in my new Malibu Beach Club bathing suit, flip-flops, and visor. I caught my reflection in the window. I looked like a total hottie, even if I did say so myself.

There was nobody in the hallway, and I couldn't help doing a little modeling strut. Pretending the corridor was a fashion-show catwalk, I took a few strides and posed like a model.

I wasn't Mary-Kate Olsen, lifeguard, anymore. Now I was Mary-Kate Olsen, supermodel, Olympic swimmer, beach goddess, and one of the "Ten Most Fascinating People of the Year."

I trailed the towel along the floor behind me and tossed my head for the imaginary photographers—

"Ahem, excuse me," said a deep voice from behind me.

"ARRGGHH!" I stepped on the back of one of my flip-flops and stumbled into the wall.

I looked up to see who had scared me and felt my mouth fall open. Talk about cute! He was a little taller than I was, with strawberry-blond hair and the bluest eyes I'd ever seen.

"Sorry! I didn't mean to startle you. Don just asked me to round up the lifeguard squad for orientation."

I was totally embarrassed. My face was probably as red as my towel. But the guy had such a sweet smile and such kind eyes, it was easy to laugh at myself. "That'll teach me to stay off the runway in fantasyland."

He grinned. "Don't worry. In *my* fantasyland, I'm the long-board champion of the world." He said it in a silly "surfer dude" voice, and we both laughed. "I gotta see if there's anybody in the office," he said. "See you outside."

Kelly came out of the locker room just as he was walking away.

"Hey!" she said. "What a cutie. He must be new. What's his name?"

"I don't know," I said, watching him disappear down the hall. But right then and there I decided I'd make it my business to find out.

❊

"Come on, Ashley. Wear the blue silk sundress," Lauren begged. "I love that."

Lauren Glazer and Brittany Bowen were Mary-Kate's and my best friends from school. They had come over to watch DVDs with Mary-Kate tonight. I was looking forward to going out with Aaron, but I was a little sorry I was going to miss the fun with my friends. Everybody had started summer jobs this week, and I wanted to hear all the news.

I shook my head. "I can't wear the blue silk sundress. I dropped ice cream on it the other day, and I haven't gotten the spot out."

"I hope you get it out in time for Nathan and Carly's wedding," Lauren said casually.

"Oh, I wouldn't wear that anyway," I said. "It's way too informal."

Lauren's light complexion turned pink. It made her freckles stand out and her blue eyes sparkle. "Really? So it's going to be a formal wedding?"

I felt like kicking myself. This was exactly the kind of thing I was *not* supposed to do.

I picked up a pillow and threw it at Lauren. "Go downstairs and help Brittany make popcorn," I ordered. "You are not getting one more scrap of information out of me."

Lauren ran from the room with a giggle. She and Brittany had been pumping me for details about Nathan and Carly's wedding ever since they arrived.

A couple of minutes later Mary-Kate came running in and threw herself across my bed. "Brittany and Lauren have popcorn *and* fudge under control." She flopped over onto her back. "I am *so* excited, Ashley. Not just about the job but about this one guy at the club. I don't know his name yet, but I'm working on it. He was on beach patrol today."

"Isn't everybody on beach patrol?" I asked. I pulled a pink cashmere halter and sweater out of the closet. It would look great with my white boot-cut jeans.

"No. The club has a huge pool for people who don't want to turn their little kids loose on the beach. Lots of lifeguards work the pool." She laughed. "My major job today was enforcing the swim-diapers-for-babies rule."

"Huh?"

"We don't want . . . anything floating around in the pool."

"Gross!" I yelled.

"You got that right. That's why babies must wear swim diapers at all times." She held up a finger as if she was quoting from a rule book.

My purple cell rang. I grabbed it.

"Hey, Ashley. It's Aaron."

"Hi! We're still on, aren't we?"

"Yeah! Of course." He sounded insulted that I'd even asked. "I'm just running a little late," he said. "Gotta get gas. I know I had all day to do that, but I just forgot. Okay?"

Boy, he was so defensive. "That's okay," I said in my nicest voice. "Take your time. Our reservation isn't till seven, right?"

There was a long silence.

"You did make a reservation, didn't you? It's a hot place. It's hard to get a table."

"It's Monday night," he argued. "Who makes reservations for a Monday night?"

I forced a smile. "You're right. Not a problem. I'm sure everything will be fine. See you soon." I hung up.

Mary-Kate gave me a funny look. "What's with the fake happiness act?"

I sighed. "Ever since we got back together after our breakup, things with Aaron have been kind of weird. It's as if he's always trying to pick a fight. When I suggest commonsense stuff like making a reservation, he acts like I'm some big control freak."

Mary-Kate groaned. "I feel so guilty about that."

"Don't. It's over. It's in the past. Well, most of it anyway."

Mary-Kate had had this great job working for *Girlz* magazine. She'd done a bunch of interviews with different couples in our school for this article on dating. Well, once she started quoting people about their relationships and printing it in the magazine, most of the couples broke up—including me and Aaron. After reading some of the things I'd said, about what was important to me in a relationship, Aaron felt we weren't right for each other and got very upset. We managed to put it back together, but things between us still weren't normal. Ever since then all the little things—like dinner reservations—had become big deals.

I picked up the green blouse I'd tried on earlier and put it back on a matching green padded hanger. "You don't think I'm a control freak, do you?"

Mary-Kate sat up. "No way! That's ridiculous. Totally *absurd.*"

This is why I love my sister.

"You're detail-oriented, that's all. A perfectionist. It's what makes you good at everything you do. I mean, how many of our friends color-code their closets? And that spreadsheet you put together that lets you track how many times you wear an outfit? That was brilliant!"

Why was I suddenly not feeling reassured?

"And just remember the Theory of Compatibility Web site you made. It was genius. You should get a Nobel Prize for that. Sure, there were a few bugs in the system, but you stuck with it till it worked. You matched up some really great couples that are still together!"

Yeah, I thought, *but I also nearly ruined everyone in the school's existing love life.* That was why I couldn't get too mad at Mary-Kate about her magazine article. The Web site I created last year had done some pretty major damage, too, even though I was really just trying to match up people with their perfect partner. But Mary-Kate was right that it had been really successful for some of our friends.

Ugh! I was an even worse control freak than I thought! I groaned. "No wonder Aaron is bummed. I'm just like Carly. Bossy and overbearing."

Oops!

I could almost see Mary-Kate's ears swivel forward like satellite dishes. "Really? Carly O'Connor is bossy and overbearing? I didn't know that. She and Nathan Richie seem like such a perfect couple. Tell me more!"

I bit my lip. Ava had told me to face the mirror every day and take the "Weddings by Ava Pledge."

RULE ONE: NEVER discuss the clients outside the office.

RULE TWO: NEVER get personally involved in the clients' lives. Meddling is completely unprofessional.

I hadn't even gotten through week one, and I was already in violation of Rule One.

Luckily Brittany and Lauren shouted for

Mary-Kate to come to the kitchen and check out the fudge. Mary-Kate bounced out of the room and thundered down the stairs.

As soon as she was gone, I faced the mirror and raised my right hand. "I, Ashley Olsen, pledge that from now on my lips are sealed on the subject of Nathan and Carly. No one will get any information out of Ashley Olsen. Not one teeny tiny single solitary shred."

chapter three

"No. Wait. Don't get off here."

"C'mon, Ashley. This is a shortcut." Aaron pulled off the freeway.

"But the road is closed," I said.

"There's a detour," he insisted.

I knew that detour had been closed since yesterday. But it looked as if Aaron and I were having one of *those* nights. Whatever I said, Aaron said the opposite.

Ten seconds later we pulled to a stop in front of a solid wall of orange barrels.

ROAD CLOSED.

Aaron threw the car into reverse and started to .back up. But before he could move ten feet, a whole string of cars had followed us right into the dead end.

Now we were blocked in from the rear.

Aaron gave me a sheepish look.

Sure, I could have said something like *I told you so!* But I decided not to take the chance of upsetting Aaron more. So instead I said, "Don't worry. I'm sure we'll be out of here in two minutes."

Famous last words.

It was an hour and a half before we got to the new beach café. Aaron was grumpy, I was starving, and the restaurant was packed.

"You don't have a reservation?" The hostess looked at us as if we were crazy. "If you want to wait, we might have a table in about two hours. But I can't guarantee anything."

Two hours! No way. We went outside and got back into the car.

Aaron started the engine. "I'm sorry, Ashley. This is my fault." He looked so sorry and embarrassed that I felt worse for him than I did for me.

"Don't sweat it. There are tons of restaurants around here. Let's just stop at the next one that looks good," I said.

He smiled happily. "Great!" That's how Aaron likes to do things. Play it by ear. Make it up as he goes along. See where the adventure takes him—that sort of thing.

Unfortunately the adventure took us to six restaurants. Every single one of them was packed. Finally we found a greasy fried-fish stand with some picnic tables outside.

We sat down at a sticky table with paper plates full of the soggiest, greasiest seafood I had ever seen.

Aaron sighed. "Sorry, Ashley. I know this isn't the evening you pictured."

I grabbed a bunch of napkins and started blotting the grease off my fish. "The important thing is that we're together." I reached for the plastic bottle of catsup. Maybe that would kill the taste of the grease.

I turned the plastic dispenser upside down and squeezed.

SPLAT!

When the catsup broke through the crusty nozzle, it shot out in every direction. Catsup landed on the table, the ground, the front of my sweater, and in my purse. Everywhere except on the fish.

I was so annoyed, I wanted to shriek. But when I saw Aaron's face, I swallowed my irritation. He looked horrified.

He dove for some napkins and started wiping up the mess. The more he wiped, the more the red goo smeared.

I took some napkins and water and tried to clean the front of my sweater. I managed to get most of it off, but I still had a big damp red stain on my cashmere sweater.

"I'm really sorry, Ashley," Aaron kept saying. "I'm so sorry."

I could see he felt really terrible.

I didn't want him to feel terrible. I wanted us to have a good time together—the way we used to. Why was it so hard? I picked up all the dirty napkins and threw them into a big trash barrel. "Would you please quit apologizing?" I begged.

"I feel like I've really let you down."

"Well, you haven't. So let's just eat our dinner and talk about something else." I took a bite of fried shrimp—at least I think it was shrimp—and asked him who he thought would wind up running for student council next year.

We talked about student politics. We talked about video games. We talked about college football. We talked about music. And no matter what I really thought, I agreed with every single thing Aaron said. I just wanted him to stop feeling bad for one night. I didn't even ask him how his job search was going. From his phone calls earlier that day, I could pretty much tell.

By the time we left, Aaron seemed to be in a better mood.

So what if I'd eaten some lousy food? So what if I'd let him do all the talking? If it made Aaron happy, it was worth it.

We got home, and Aaron walked me to the door. He stood really close to me. My heart began to pound. Kissing Aaron was like being in heaven.

I closed my eyes and waited.

And waited.

And waited.

Nothing.

I opened my eyes.

Aaron had this funny look on his face. Half mad. Half sad. Half embarrassed. (I know that doesn't add up, but I never said I was good at fractions.)

"It's no use," he said quietly.

"What's no use?"

"I can't make this work anymore," he said. "We're just too different."

I felt my face go hot, then cold, then hot again. What was I hearing?

"I feel like . . . I don't know . . . like you're talking down to me. It's like you think nobody but you can do anything right."

"That's not true!" I cried.

"I'm not saying it's true. I'm just saying that's how I feel. I don't like feeling that way. So I guess . . ." He let my fingers slip out of his hands. "I guess I want to break up."

He kissed me quickly on the cheek, then turned and walked back to his car.

I couldn't believe it. I couldn't believe this was happening. Aaron was breaking up with me.

I felt my throat tighten as he got into his car. I

had done everything I knew how to make things work.

What was I supposed to do now? Run after him and apologize?

Or go into the house, slam the door, and wait for *him* to apologize?

Something hot fell on my hand. I looked down. It was a shining tear.

I fiercely wiped my eyes.

What did this boy want from me? And what was I supposed to apologize for?

✿

"Ashley, it can't be true. You imagined the whole thing. It was a bad dream or something. What did you eat last night?" I stared at Ashley's face, hoping she was kidding.

"He was serious, Mary-Kate," Ashley said. "And I don't even want to think about what I ate last night. *That* was a nightmare. Unfortunately, I was one hundred percent awake."

"How could anybody break up with someone as beautiful, smart, funny, and nice as you? It doesn't make sense."

Ashley was driving me to work in the pink Mustang we share. It was a gift from Mom and Dad on our sixteenth birthday. We had the top down, and it was one of those sunny California days that made any bad news seem sort of unreal.

"I just don't know what to do." Ashley sighed after she finished telling me the whole story.

"Why don't you wait a couple of days and see what happens?" I suggested. "Aaron sounds like he's just mad at the world right now. Probably because he's stuck at home watching TV while everybody else is doing cool stuff. He'll probably land some great job in a couple of days. Then he'll be sorry he was such a jerk."

Ashley pulled up in front of the beach club to let me off. "You think so?"

Poor Ashley. She looked so sad. "I know so!" I gave her a hug and hopped out of the car. "I wish you could come to work with me instead of going to Ava's. Gorgeous day. Gorgeous beach. Gorgeous guys. Who could stay unhappy for long?"

She laughed. "Fortunately I like my job—so far. Gorgeous clients. Gorgeous clothes. Gorgeous places. But some days are definitely better than others." Ashley waved and pulled out of the drive.

I was a bit early, so I took the long way into the club—around the tennis courts. I could hear the soft *bop, bop* of tennis balls. The tennis players tended to be at the club early, since it was sometimes too hot to play in the middle of the day.

I walked past the pro shop and drooled over the warm-up suits for sale. I knew where my first paycheck was going.

I checked in at the office and dropped my gear off in the locker room. The lifeguard squad was assembling in the pool area, so that's where I headed. I still didn't know the cute guy's name, but I was determined to at least have a conversation with him today.

When I joined Kelly in the group, I saw him standing at the far end, so I began inching my way in his direction as soon as Don blew his whistle to signal we were starting. Kelly gave me a wink.

Don wore a red-and-white baseball cap with his name embroidered over the Malibu Beach Club logo. "Good morning, everyone. Before we start today, we're going to do a few brush-up exercises. . . ."

I casually took a few steps to the left. I was getting close to the cute guy. A couple more steps and I would be right next to him.

". . . I know you've all been through training, but it never hurts to review. . . ."

Aha! I was right beside him. And it all seemed one hundred percent casual and accidental. Am I good or what?

". . . We'll start by reviewing some of the holds we use on drowning victims. Your partner will be whoever happens to be standing next to you."

I felt my heart go *BOOINNGGG!* That meant my partner was the cute guy—whose name I still

34

didn't know. Luckily, Don started calling the roll. I'd know his name soon. He called the roll military style. "Adams, Lyle. Addison, Kareem. Culotta, Brandt . . ."

I watched the cute guy out of the corner of my eye. I was getting impatient. Don was already up to the *K*'s, and I still had no useful information.

"Lopez, Paul. Lucky, Dave . . ."

That's when the cute guy shouted, "Here!"

Everybody including Don began to laugh at how his name sounded. *Lucky Dave*.

"How do I get assigned to 'Lucky Dave's' shifts?" someone called out. "I'm superstitious, and I like the sound of his name."

Everybody began to joke about how nothing could go wrong when you had somebody named "Lucky Dave" on your squad.

After all the laughing and kidding died down, Don went on with roll call. After I answered to my name, Lucky Dave turned toward me. "Finally I know your name!"

So! He'd been curious about me, too. This was good.

Don blew his whistle. "Everybody into the pool."

We all dog-paddled for a while, then started pulling one another around the pool in some of the standard holds.

Dave Lucky had one arm wrapped around me with his hand cupped under my chin. He looked down at me. "Some days I really do feel like Lucky Dave." It was the same silly "surfer dude" voice he'd used the other day. "It's not even nine in the morning, and I've already got my hands on a cute girl in a bathing suit."

I laughed so hard, I sucked water into my nose and went under. Not exactly smooth.

I came back up, still laughing and coughing.

Don blew his whistle. "Come on, guys. No horsing around. I need you to take this seriously."

"Sorry," we both said. I dove under so Don wouldn't see the ridiculously huge grin I had on my face.

I was totally thrilled. The connection was definitely there. I couldn't wait to find out what would happen next!

chapter four

"No horseplay!" I shouted at two kids wrestling in the shallow end of the pool. They immediately broke apart.

Such power! I hoped it wouldn't go to my head.

A young mom started into the pool with her baby. Uh-oh! The baby wasn't wearing a swim diaper.

I didn't feel comfortable blowing the whistle at a grown-up. So I tapped her on the shoulder and politely reminded her about the swim-diaper rule.

Her face fell. "But I don't have any."

"No problem. If you go to the office, they'll be happy to give you some."

Okay. So it wasn't exactly *Baywatch*. Being assigned to the pool wasn't nearly as cool as being assigned to the beach. But it was still fun.

Besides, Lucky Dave was assigned to the pool

area, too. My eyes flickered around the perimeter of the pool. Aha! There he was at the other end—and he was looking right at me.

Major eye contact.

My whole stomach fluttered.

Did I say pool duty wasn't exciting? I must have been nuts.

Ten minutes later I thought I was even more nuts when I saw Lucky Dave heading around the pool toward me.

"Take your break with me in half an hour?"

"After that hold you put on me this morning, how could I say no? Uh-oh. Did I just say that out loud?"

Lucky Dave laughed. "It's a date."

Things were definitely getting more interesting by the minute.

✽

I'd picked up coffee, but Greg wasn't at Ooh La Latte after all. That was okay, because I wasn't exactly in the mood to flirt. I was totally bummed about Aaron.

As soon as I walked into Ava's though, the creative energy there perked me right up. Gorgeous fabric swatches were everywhere. A dining table was set with a bunch of different sample place settings—all of them beautiful. There were fresh flowers in every vase.

Ava looked up and gave me a distracted smile. She was on the phone and checking her style guide for the O'Connor–Richie wedding. A style guide was a thick notebook she assembled for each wedding. It had all the sketches, drawings, contacts, flower arrangements, everything needed for the wedding, including any ideas or clippings the couple had provided—such as a close-up shot of Carly's mother's eyes so we could match Lila O'Connor's flowers to them. I knew Ava would go fully digital someday, but in the meantime the guide was her bible.

"Yes . . . yes . . . yes . . ." she was saying. "We can guarantee payment in advance. That's no problem. We just need you to guarantee delivery. I know three thousand tulips is a lot of tulips. . . . Yes . . . all pink. Very good. Thank you."

She hung up and ran a hand over her smooth bob. "Carly's going to be here any minute now. And she's bringing her sister, Lenore. We're going to get Lenore's measurements for her bridesmaid dress. Then I'm headed for Los Angeles to check out a new photographer. Here's your list of stuff to do."

I looked at the list. It was hard to feel over-worked when your to-do list sent you to a major jewelry store to look at pearl bracelets for brides-maids. What fun!

The door opened, and suddenly it was as if Carly and two clones had arrived—and they were all talking at once. "Ava, Ashley, this is my sister, Lenore, and my mother, Lila."

Carly's mom hardly looked older than Carly. She was beautiful, and I could see where Carly had gotten her dramatic flair. Lila wore a big hat with a huge bow on it. And her eyes were a deep, deep blue. Lenore looked like Carly, too, but smaller. My size, actually.

There was a lot of air kissing and exclaiming. Carly showed Lila the sketches and photos.

"This is where we're getting married," Carly said, showing her mother the photos of the three-hundred-year-old winery tucked away in the hills.

"It's wonderful, darling. It looks like a castle."

"Well, of course it does, Mother. I wouldn't settle for anything less."

Everybody laughed, and Lenore winked at me while Ava took her measurements and jotted them on a piece of paper.

Finally Carly grabbed her mom and Lenore by the arm. "No more talking," she said bossily. "We're going to lunch with my agent. If we don't hurry, we'll be late." Carly blew us a kiss. "I forgot the additions to the guest list. But Nathan said he'll bring them over later this morning."

And they were gone. Ava and I looked at each

other and laughed. They'd only been in the office for a few minutes, but we felt as if we'd been through a hurricane.

Ava shook her head. "I've got to go, too. You wait for Nathan, then head for the jeweler. I'll call you on your cell in a couple of hours, and we'll figure out the rest of the day."

Ava opened the desk and took something out. "Here."

I held out my hand.

She placed a key in my palm. "Here's your key. Always make sure you lock the door behind you when you let yourself in or when you leave."

My mouth opened and closed. I didn't know what to say. It was such an incredible display of trust, it gave me a lump in my throat.

Ava smiled and closed my fingers over the key. "See you later." She threw a hot pink pashmina stole over her black tank top and short leather skirt—she was always stylish—and left.

Suddenly I felt as if fresh starts were in the stars. Something was bothering Aaron, but he'd get over it, and he'd be sorry. By tomorrow, maybe even tonight, we'd be kissing and making up. I just knew it.

Ring!

It was Aaron. It had to be. Even though it was the office line and not my cell. I picked up the phone before it could ring twice. "Weddings by Ava. Ashley speaking."

"Hi, Ashley. It's Aaron."

Yes! I silently pumped my fist with relief.

I sat down and waited for him to apologize—trying to decide if I would let him make it up to me with dinner or whether I would also require flowers.

"Listen, after I got home, I realized I have a couple of your favorite CDs in my car. I thought you might be uncomfortable calling me about them, so I wanted to let you know. I'll get them back to you as soon as possible."

It was a total slap in the face. He was basically saying *"You'll never be in my car again—so I for sure don't need your favorite CDs taking up space."*

"Ashley? Are you there?"

How could he be so cruel? He seemed to be going out of his way to make it hurt even more. No way would I give him the satisfaction of letting him know he'd hurt me. I forced the lump out of my throat.

"I'm here. Just trying to juggle six things at once—as usual." I laughed gaily. "No problem. Just drop them off whenever."

"I've also got some magazines that are yours. I'll get those back to you, too."

"Great! Listen, gotta run. Nathan and Carly are

picking me up any minute now for breakfast at the Dolphin Hotel." I crossed my fingers at the lie. "Then I've got to do some shopping around Beverly Hills."

"Okay, then. Well . . . uh . . ."

I could tell he was trying to think of something besides "see you soon" to use as a sign-off.

"Bye," I managed to choke out. I put the phone down a split second before I burst into tears.

I couldn't help it. I'd never felt so hurt in my whole life. I reached for the box of tissues and grabbed a wad.

Then I cried long enough to melt my mascara, which caused my upper lashes to fuse with my lower lashes. I pulled a little pocket mirror from the desk drawer.

Ugh! My nose was red and huge. My eyes were swollen slits. And I had eyeliner running down to my chin.

I'd never looked worse in my life.

So of course that's when somebody knocked on the front door.

chapter five

I looked out the peephole.

Oh, no! Nathan Richie! How totally humiliating to have a handsome movie star see me looking like a watery vampire.

"Ashley? Are you in there?"

"Uh . . . can you wait two seconds?"

His voice was tense. "Not really. I think there's a reporter right behind me. Can you let me in now?"

What could I do? I opened the door, and Nathan slipped in, shutting the door tightly behind him. "I know reporters are my best friends, but right now I'm just not in the mood. All I want to do is drop this stuff off for Carly and—"

He broke off when he saw my face. "Whoa! What happened?"

"Nothing," I answered, even though I knew that sounded completely stupid.

He put his hands on my shoulders and looked at me. "I know that is *not* a happy face."

I blew my nose. "It's . . . It's . . . It's not your problem. Let's not talk about it. Please."

"I've only seen a face like that when there's a breakup going on. Did you break up with him, or did he break up with you?" He went into the kitchenette, got a glass of water, and brought it back to me.

"He broke up with me."

"Then he's got problems, and you're better off without him," Nathan said.

I couldn't help laughing. "That's what my sister says."

"Your sister is right." He grinned. "Carly broke up with me once. I cried for two days and looked just like you look now." He grabbed a tissue and wiped my cheeks. "Luckily I wasn't wearing mascara."

I smiled. "So did you think she had . . . problems, and you were better off without her?"

He laughed. "No. I thought my life was over."

I took the tissue from him and continued the cleanup on my own. "How did you two get back together?"

"We both came to our senses. We realized that we didn't have to be alike to be in love." He smiled. "Listen, if it's meant to be, you'll get back together. If not, you and the right guy will still hook up someday. And when that guy comes along, you'll be totally happy—like I am."

His phone rang. He checked the Caller ID, frowned, then pressed the TALK button. "Hi! What'd you find out?"

Whoever was on the other end talked for a long time. The longer that person talked, the more Nathan's face fell.

"So there's *nothing* you can do?" Nathan's shoulders sagged. "Okay, then. Thanks. Yeah. Bye." He clicked off and stared into space for a long time.

"It's none of my business, but that's not a happy face either," I said. "Do you want tissues, water, or both?"

He smiled bleakly. "Nothing. I'm fine. It was just some business stuff."

"Nothing to do with the wedding, I hope."

"I don't think so."

"Huh?"

"Sorry. Sorry. I shouldn't have said that."

"Please tell me. Please. It'll make me feel a little better."

He ran his hands through his hair while he thought about it. With a sigh he dropped into a nearby chair. "You know this movie Carly and I are supposed to be in together?"

46

I nodded. "Yeah. The Army picture, right?"

He shook his head. "It *was* an Army movie fifty rewrites ago. Now it's about the Navy."

"And . . . that's bad?"

"That's very bad," he said.

"How come?"

He pressed his lips together. "Well . . . because . . . it's bad . . . because Nathan Richie, America's Number One Box Office Action-Adventure Hero, cannot swim."

Nathan's confession caught me off guard. I know it's always easy to think other people's problems are no big deal. But this really *didn't* sound like a big deal to me. "Can't you use a swim double or something?"

"Are you kidding? If anybody found out, I'd look like a total fool. The tabloids would skewer me. But that's nothing compared to what Carly would do to me. She's an amazing athlete. She can do anything. And she expects me to be able to do anything, too. She would totally lose respect for me. How could she marry a man she doesn't respect?"

"No way!" I cried, dismissing the thought with a wave of a hand. "Carly would never lose respect for you just because you can't swim."

"No. But you see the problem is . . . I told her I *could* swim."

"You mean you lied?"

"I thought my agent could get the script changed. Who knew it would come to this?" He looked at me. "You know what broke us up before? I didn't tell her the truth about something."

He puffed out his cheeks and then let out a long sigh. "I thought I'd learned my lesson. But it just seemed like . . . I don't know . . ."

He rubbed his forehead. "You have to promise you won't tell anybody. I'm figuring that you can keep a secret because you work for Ava. But you still have to promise me to keep this quiet till I can work things out."

You know all that corny stuff they say about how helping others takes your mind off your own problems? Well, it's true. I felt my mouth curve into a huge smile.

"Nathan Richie," I announced, "you came to the right place. It just so happens that I have a *brilliant* idea!"

chapter six

"No way!"

"Way!"

"You actually ate a ladybug?"

"I was two. What did I know about fine dining? I probably thought it was a tiny polka-dotted M&M."

Lucky Dave and I were walking the beach during our break. We were headed for the little boats that were used for rescues. Don had suggested that we familiarize ourselves with the club's equipment. While we walked there, Dave was keeping me laughing with stories of himself as a kid at this same beach club.

We arrived at the boats. Kareem and Kelly were looking over the life vests and ropes. Kelly gave us a big smile. "It almost makes you hope somebody calls for help, doesn't it? I'm dying to take one of these babies out."

"Don says he's going to take us out one by one and run us through the drill again," Kareem said.

"Cool!" Dave and I both said. Then we smiled at each other. I was psyched we were so in sync!

The beach was starting to get crowded. There were swimmers in the shallow water and lots of surfers way out where the waves were breaking.

Four members of the squad sat in the lofty lifeguard chairs, watching the surfers through binoculars. Four more squad members were positioned on the ground, to watch the swimmers.

Several yards away I saw my friend Danielle and her mom. They were stretched out in beach chairs and wearing sunglasses.

Danielle's mom was a big movie star, so I should have figured they were club members. Danielle and her mom spotted me and waved. I waved back but resisted running over to them. I was feeling very cool and professional.

Suddenly the PA system sprang to life with a rattle. "Attention, Malibu Beach Club members and staff. Reminder: There will be a beach party and bonfire on Friday night. Everyone is invited and encouraged to bring friends."

Everybody on the beach cheered. Dave and I grinned at each other. What a perfect time to make my move. I leaned a tiny bit forward, getting ready to suggest that we go together.

But before I could get the words out of my mouth, Don came up behind us. "I need you guys to go back to the pool area," he said. "It's really getting crowded."

"Okay," we both said.

He put a hand up in front of Dave. "Dave, hold up two seconds, and let's go over your shift schedule for next week."

Kareem, Kelly, and I walked back down the beach and into the enclosed pool area.

I positioned myself so that I could keep an eye on the pool area entryway and maybe catch Dave when he came back.

I watched for what seemed like ten minutes. Wasn't he ever coming?

Something at the corner of my eye caught my attention. I turned and saw the toddler from this morning. He was wearing a swim diaper. Good. But he was standing right on the edge of the deep end and teetering forward.

Where was his mom?

I didn't think. I dove. My hand closed over the toddler's arm one nanosecond before he could fall forward into the water. He let out a happy scream, probably thinking we were playing a game.

His mom was over by the tables blowing up some floaties. When she heard the scream, she looked up.

I'll never forget the expression on her face when

51

she realized what could have happened to her son. She dropped the floats and came running over to us.

"Thank you!" she gasped, grabbing her baby. "I didn't see . . . I didn't realize . . . I wasn't watching for a second and—" She broke off and pressed her face into her baby's neck.

I doubt that anybody else around the pool even noticed what was going on. That just goes to show you how fast things can happen.

My legs started shaking. It wasn't so bad that the baby's mom had gotten distracted. Things like that happen. That's why pools have lifeguards.

What was upsetting me was that *I* had gotten distracted. *I* was the lifeguard. *I* was the one who was supposed to be paying attention.

If I'd been doing my job, that baby never would have gotten so close to the water.

I swallowed, feeling totally ashamed. I was so busy trying to flirt, I had endangered a life.

Never again. From that second on I was going to keep my eyes on the pool and *only* the pool.

For the next hour I was like a hawk. Nothing distracted me. Nothing. Not even Dave Lucky.

"Hey, Mary-Kate, I'm going to the break room. You coming?"

I didn't look up at him because I didn't want to take my eyes off the water. "I don't really need a break. But I'll meet up with you in a bit, okay?" I said without ever really paying attention to him.

Some little kids were climbing the ladder for the high dive. I shot off toward the deep end in case they got into any trouble.

For the rest of my shift I was the most careful and alert lifeguard the Malibu Beach Club had ever seen. I stood at the rim of the pool with my eyes glued to the water.

"Mary-Kate, want a drink?" I cut my eyes sideways. It was Dave again, holding two bottles of water from the snack shack.

Before I could answer, I saw two kids running along the walkway that led from the pool area to the beach. I didn't see any grown-ups with them. I sprinted in their direction. "Hey, kids!"

They stopped.

"Where are your parents?"

They stared at me with big scared eyes.

I pointed toward the pool. "Sorry, guys. No kids on the beach without an adult." I tried to look really stern and scary. "Don't let me catch you sneaking onto the beach again!"

They turned and ran toward the pool. I blew my whistle. They froze and looked back.

"No running," I reminded them.

They power-walked away as fast as their little legs could carry them. It was hard not to laugh. They looked like very nervous ducklings.

I heard three whistle blasts. That meant Kelly had arrived by the pool to take my shift. I returned the three blasts—which meant I was going off duty.

I looked around for Dave. He wasn't by the pool, so I walked up and down the beach to see if I could find him.

The sand was covered with bright towels, umbrellas, teenagers, and families. Somebody was playing salsa music, and at the far end of the beach some teenagers were dancing.

It looked as if everybody was having fun. I ran my eyes over the water. No sign of trouble. No sign of Dave either.

I went to the break room. Kareem and Lyle were playing a computer game. "Anybody seen Dave?" I asked.

"He signed out about fifteen minutes ago," Kareem answered. "He's gone."

Darn! I checked my watch. I was supposed to be gone, too. I hurried to the locker room, changed my clothes, and went out front.

I spotted the pink Mustang and waved at Ashley. I jumped in. "So? How was your day?" I asked. "Anything new on the Aaron front?"

She pulled a face. "Only that he seems completely determined to break up with me. But let's not talk about that now. I have something really important to ask you."

"Okay. Shoot."

"How would you like to do a little swim coaching?"

"Does 'ugh' answer your question?"

"But what if you were coaching a famous movie star?"

That got my attention. "What famous movie star?"

"Nathan Richie."

"I think we'd better put the top up. The sun is doing something to your brain. Why would Nathan Richie want swim coaching from me?"

Ashley smiled and accelerated onto the freeway. "I'm going to tell you. But you have to promise never to tell anyone. Ever."

❋

Okay. So now I, Ashley Olsen, had broken Rule Two of the "Wedding by Ava Pledge." NEVER meddle in the clients' private lives. But rules were meant to be broken, right?

Besides, I wasn't *meddling*. I was *helping*. I was helping everybody, including Ava.

At least that's what I told myself as I headed up to my room. Mary-Kate and I had just gotten home. I was glad we'd had Nathan to talk about. Otherwise it would have been hard not to tell her about my trip to Baubles to scope out pearl bracelets for Carly's bridesmaids. Or my trip to

Let Them Eat Cake to sample their luscious lemon-chocolate-raspberry soufflé wedding cake. Or my quick visit to Scents and Sensibility to scout fragrances for the guests' hotel suites.

By the time I reached the end of my to-do list, it had been a great day, and I hadn't thought about Aaron for hours.

Just as I hit my room, I noticed my cell phone had a message waiting. I retrieved it.

"Hi, Ashley. This is Aaron. Listen, I'm getting your stuff together and . . . um . . . you've got some of my stuff, too. That book about ancient Egypt and my blue jacket. Could you give me a call when you've got it together so we can decide where and when we should meet?"

"*Oh!*" I screamed. It was all I could do not to throw the phone against the wall. He must've tried while I was on a call—one of many—with Ava.

Mary-Kate stuck her head into my room. "What's wrong?"

"Aaron. He's going out of his way to make sure I know he's serious about breaking up."

"What now?"

"He wants his stuff back."

"What stuff?"

I narrowed my eyes. "What an *excellent* question. He asked for it. Now he's going to get it. *All* of it."

56

chapter seven

Wouldn't you know? The next morning cars were parked all up and down the street. I had to leave the Mustang practically a block away from Ava's.

I pulled the big cardboard box out of the backseat. In it was every single thing Aaron had ever given me.

Every book. Every CD. Every card. Every note. All those dumb refrigerator magnets. The teddy bear with the *I Love Ashley* T-shirt. Dried flowers from one of our first post-breakup dates. Fortunes from all the fortune cookies we had opened together. Horoscopes he had cut out of the paper and poked through the vents of my locker. Everything.

No way was I going to give him the satisfaction of my calling him or stopping by his house. I was taking this junk to the office, where I could pack it up and send it to him by mail.

I lugged the heavy box along the sidewalk,

getting madder with every step. I decided to stop at Ooh La Latte to get a cup of coffee.

I balanced the box on my hip and tried to pull the door open.

BAM! Somebody came barreling out. It was Greg Johnson. He ran right into me. I dropped the box, and the contents scattered across the sidewalk.

I knelt down and scrambled to pick everything up before it blew away or rolled into the street.

Greg bent down and started trying to pick things up. "Ashley! I'm so sorry. I didn't see you. Seems like you always have your hands a little too full. What do you do when I'm not around to help?"

I didn't answer. I was too angry and too upset.

He picked up the little teddy bear. When he spoke, his voice was serious. "Uh-oh. This looks like a breakup. I'm really sorry."

I snatched the bear out of his hand and threw it into the box. "Well, don't be. I'm not, and neither is he."

I reached for some magnets and froze. Right in front of my face I saw two pairs of familiar feet. Nobody wore platforms that high except Brittany. And nobody would wear toenail polish that color except Lauren.

I looked up. Lauren and Brittany were standing right there.

"Ashley, what happened? Are you okay?" Brittany asked.

I was totally embarrassed. I mean, there I was—hot, red-faced, flustered, and kneeling on the sidewalk by a box of junk. And a totally cute guy was staring at one of my stuffed animals. "I'm okay. . . . What are you guys doing here?"

"Shopping. What else? We just got our first paychecks, and we're checking out the sales," Brittany said, kneeling down to help us.

Lauren eyed my *I love Ashley* bear. "Did something happen with you and Aaron?" she asked.

I threw the last of Aaron's stuff into the box and stood. "This isn't exactly how I planned to tell you guys. But we broke up. And he asked for all his stuff back."

Greg stood up, too. He looked sort of embarrassed. "Sorry to . . . interrupt. . . ." he said. "I'll just . . . you know . . ." He trailed off and retreated into the café.

Brittany and Lauren gave me a surprised look. "Is *he* why you're breaking up?"

"Him? No! *No!* I hardly know him. Aaron and I broke up because things just were *not* working."

"But you're *perfect* for each other," Lauren protested.

Brittany twirled one of her chin-length curls. "I

thought your computer program even proved scientifically that you and Aaron were a good match."

Lauren pointed at the café. "Let's get you some coffee and you can tell us everything."

I sighed. "I wish I could, but I can't. If I stop for coffee now, I'll be late for work."

"When can we get together?"

"I'm not sure," I said, looking at my watch. I was definitely running late.

"You know about the Malibu Beach Club party, right? Why don't you plan to come with us?" Lauren suggested. "You can tell us all about it then."

It was pretty hard to think about partying at a time like this. "I'll think about it and call you later," I said. "Right now I just need a little space."

Brittany nodded, and her curls bounced. "Sure, Ashley. But you know"—she touched my arm lightly—"we're here for you."

"Thanks, guys." I heaved the box back onto my hip. I knew they meant well, but I just couldn't talk anymore.

I hurried to Ava's. The door was locked, so I let myself in with my key. No sign of Ava, but I knew she'd already been in because there was a long to-do list on my desk.

I was glad Ava wasn't there. I needed a little time alone.

I dropped the box on the floor and started the morning routine. A few minutes later somebody knocked softly at the door.

I opened the door a crack. "Greg!"

He held out a sack from the Ooh La Latte Café. "French roast with half-and-half. Your friends said it's your favorite."

I opened the door slowly. He leaned forward so I could take the bag.

"Thanks. Sorry I was so rude. I wasn't mad at you. I was . . ."

"I know," he said.

I looked at my watch. "Aren't you late for work?"

"My dad's not a real strict boss. He really just wants me to have a good time while I'm in town."

"You don't live here?"

He shook his head. "My folks are divorced. During the school year I live with my mom in New York City. I'm here to spend the summer with just my dad.

"Listen," he went on. "I know you just broke up with your boyfriend. And I don't want you to think I'm coming on too strong. But I don't really know anybody here. Sooo . . . do you think we could get together and do something sometime?"

I wasn't really ready to date anybody yet, but Greg was just too sweet. I remembered the party at the club that my best friends had just reminded me about, and I decided to take a shot. After all, he was only going to be around for the summer, right?

"My sister is a lifeguard at the Malibu Beach Club. They're having a bonfire and beach party Friday night, and a lot of my friends will be there. Would you like to come with me?"

He grinned. "Perfect!"

Perfect was turning into the key word for the day, I decided.

chapter eight

"Ashley! Wait up!"

I turned and saw Melanie Han running toward Greg and me. It was Friday night. The moon was full. The fire was high. And there were tons of people at the party. Greg was meeting a lot of my friends and he seemed to be having fun.

Melanie came over panting from her run through the sand. She wore a bikini top with low-rise flared jeans and a leather belt with a big bronze buckle. She looked totally hip. "Greg Johnson," I said, "meet Melanie Han. Her dad is, like, the fashion guru of the world."

Greg smiled. "Great. I always like to know who to call in case of a fashion emergency."

Melanie laughed. "Believe it or not, some of my friends actually do that." She grabbed my arm. "Ashley, I *had* to tell you. My dad is just so jealous of you. He said to tell you he'll bring you back anything you want from the fall fashion shows if you'll just tell him what Carly O'Connor is planning to wear at her wedding."

We both laughed. Melanie's dad made regular trips to Milan, Paris, and every other fashion hot spot in the world. Melanie had inherited his fashion flair, and, as a matter of fact, she and I had been head-to-head competitors in a recent fashion-trend-spotting contest.

"Tell your dad I am totally immune to bribes," I joked. I saw Melanie's face fall. "I've even been offered backstage passes to the next Rave concert in exchange for information."

Melanie's eyes widened, and she whistled. "Good thing I don't know any secrets. I don't think I could hold out. Not against an offer of backstage passes to Rave."

Somebody ran by Melanie just then and dumped a cup of ice down her back. With a shriek she took off after her "attacker."

I turned to Greg, but just then Jake Impenna, one of Aaron's friends, came over and pulled me aside. "I heard you and Aaron broke up. Is that true?"

"Yep. But, hey . . . these things happen." I tried to sound breezy. If he reported back to Aaron, I wanted him to say how well I was doing.

"Yeah, but you guys were such a great couple

and—" He broke off, suddenly noticing Greg standing next to me.

Jake looked a little surprised. But instead of explaining that Greg was just a friend, I decided it wouldn't hurt to have Aaron know I wasn't sitting around waiting to hear from him. And Greg fit the scenario perfectly.

Greg sensed the tension and knew exactly what to do. He gently touched my arm. "Let's get a soda," he said. We wandered off toward the coolers, got sodas, and then walked down the beach. A group of kids were playing volleyball by torchlight. Farther down some people were dancing.

We sat down on a big piece of driftwood and watched the waves. Even though we sat in silence, it didn't feel weird. Greg was easy to be with, and he was really good at keeping my mind off other things.

If this were a date—which it wasn't—I'd consider it a success.

Greg took a sip of his soda. "So, this Aaron guy. Is he here?"

"I haven't seen him," I answered.

"Think he stayed away because he thought you might be here?"

I nodded. "Probably." Aaron would have received my box in the mail by now. He must've gotten the hint.

There was a long silence. Greg moved his feet around in the sand, making little mounds. "Do you think it'll take you a long time to get over him?"

I looked up. Greg gave me a crooked grin. "Because I was just thinking that . . . you know . . . in the meantime you might want to go out with somebody. And . . ." He trailed off.

"And . . . ?" I prompted. I thought it was cute how nervous he seemed, and I knew what he was about to say.

He ran a hand through his hair. "Well, I thought maybe you'd go out with me."

Finally!

Aaron and I were over.

Greg was cute. And thoughtful. And funny.

Why not? I thought.

"Well?" he prompted.

I smiled. "Perfect!"

THUNK!

OUCH! The Frisbee smacked me right in the head.

"Mary-Kate! What is *with* you?"

I was playing Frisbee with Malcolm Freeman and his girlfriend, Sophie Curtis. This was the third time I'd been looking at the water when the Frisbee came my way.

"Sorry, guys. I just can't seem to take myself off lifeguard duty."

Malcolm retrieved the disk. "All work and no play make Mary-Kate a very bad Frisbee player."

"I can't help it. Something really scary happened a couple of days ago, and it's still bothering me." I told Sophie and Malcolm about how I'd almost missed seeing the toddler heading for the water.

"Wow!" Sophie said. "That would bother me, too. What was going on? How come you didn't notice? Too many kids in the pool?"

I shrugged. I didn't want to tell them it was because I was trying to scope out Lucky Dave. And speaking of Dave, where was he?

I looked at the various groups of people in the moonlight. I saw Melanie, Lauren, and Brittany talking to Jake and some other guys I didn't know. Ashley was off to one side, sitting and talking with the legal assistant she'd introduced me to. He seemed a bit older than the guys we usually hung with, but Ashley said he was in high school, too, so I guess he was a senior or something. She looked like she was having a great time.

I saw Kelly Mason and Kareem Addison heading into the shallow surf with boogie boards. Out of habit my eyes flew to the lifeguard chairs. They were manned. Good.

I felt a tap on my shoulder. I turned. Talk about

good timing. "Lucky Dave! I was looking for you!"

"Hey," he said. "I just got here."

I introduced Dave to Malcolm and Sophie, then excused myself from the Frisbee game.

"Have you eaten yet?" Dave asked.

"No. Come on, let's get something."

The amount of food at the party was incredible. There was a huge selection of Hawaiian chicken on skewers, meatballs with cilantro, spring rolls, and—of course—hamburgers and hot dogs.

"No ladybugs," Dave said sadly.

"Ladybugs are expensive this time of year," I joked.

I could see more people heading into the waves for a night swim. Even though I knew there were lifeguards on duty, it was still hard to relax.

We grazed for a while, laughing and talking. It was fun, but I wished we weren't at the beach club. I just couldn't loosen up. I could feel my gaze constantly wandering to the water, to the pool area, and over to the surfboard rack. Sometimes Dave had to ask me something more than once.

We headed down the beach to where people were dancing. A ballad was playing.

"Want to dance?" Dave asked.

I was a little shy dancing a slow dance, but when Dave put his arms around me, I felt totally comfortable. We swayed a little to the music. It was nice, but almost immediately the music switched to some up-tempo surfer music.

We backed away from each other and started dancing faster. It was a great song, and pretty soon half the beach party was dancing. We formed a samba line and snaked along the sand.

Out of the corner of my eye I thought I saw some trouble in the shallows. Some people were thrashing around, and I saw a hand waving. I broke away from the samba line and ran down the beach to get a closer look.

Of course there was no problem. It was just Danielle, Noah Atkins, and Jake Impenna having a water fight. Once they spotted me, Danielle and Jake ran up, grabbed me by the arms, and started dragging me toward the water.

"No! No!" I wanted to get back to Dave. "Let me go!" I yelled, but I was laughing, too.

They paid no attention. Soon I was soaked. "Okay! That *does* it, Danielle!" I grabbed a nearby boogie board, angled it just so, and sent a tidal wave of water in her direction. The next thing I knew, we were in the middle of a huge water fight.

Ten minutes later I slopped back out of the water. I searched the dancing group but didn't see Dave anywhere.

I looked up and down the beach. No sign of him.

Finally I spotted Dave from the back—just as he disappeared through the club exit into the parking lot.

chapter nine

"Ashley! I've got good news, and I've got bad news." Ava was always so dramatic. "The good news is that you did a great job on the research for those bracelets. I sent the digital pictures to Carly to review. She likes them."

"Great!" I said, turning away from the computer.

Ava gave me a thumbs-up. "Now the bad news. Carly's changed her mind again. She doesn't want white horses—she wants black. And no carriages *or* buggies. The bridal party will ride on horseback. That means sidesaddles for the bridesmaids."

"Sidesaddles!"

"Sidesaddles."

"Who rides sidesaddle anymore?"

"Carly does," Ava said, gulping down two aspirin. "She learned to ride sidesaddle for a movie about some ancient Scottish warrior queen."

"Yeah, but how many of her bridesmaids can ride that way?"

Ava pinched the bridge of her nose, as if she was getting a migraine. "Carly says if she can learn how to ride sidesaddle, so can her brides-maids."

It was so absurd, I didn't know what to say. How were they to learn—*where* were they to learn—without attracting any attention? They were all pretty famous women around town.

"Carly's going to Europe for a couple of weeks with her mother and sister. She wants all the details nailed down by the time she gets back. So you'd better get on the Internet and find some sidesaddles. If they're not available through saddle shops, check the prop departments of some of the film studios. See if we can rent some."

I swiveled back toward the computer.

"Oh!" she said. "And line up the best hair extensionist in Hollywood."

"For Carly?"

Ava nodded. "As soon as she gets back, they're going to start mapping the water stunts for the new movie. So she's getting her hair cut short in Paris, but she wants long hair for the wedding."

I hit the keyboard running. I had a lot to do.

But mainly I was thinking about Nathan. I'd thought maybe he was worrying too much about his not-being-able-to-swim thing. But now I thought differently.

A woman who expected her bridesmaids to be able to ride sidesaddle would for sure expect her fiancé to be able to swim.

Good thing Project Learn To Swim was swinging into action today. In fact, Mary-Kate would be arriving at Nathan's house just about now.

✿

I was totally nervous when I got to Nathan Richie's huge house. I rang the bell and tried to look confident.

I thought maybe a butler would answer the door. And that all kinds of assistants would be buzzing around. But Nathan opened the door himself wearing a T-shirt and some swim trunks.

He smiled. "Hi, Mary-Kate! Come in. Nice to meet you."

I walked into the front hall. The place was really pretty, but suprisingly there was hardly any furniture.

"We're buying a house together after the wedding," he explained, noticing my look around. "I figured, why buy a bunch of stuff that she would only make me get rid of later?"

I'd seen almost all Nathan Richie's movies, and it was kind of strange to think that anybody could *make* this action-adventure hero do anything. But

Ashley had said he was nuts about Carly. I guess she was right.

"Want something to drink?" he offered.

"No thanks."

"How about a sandwich?"

"I already ate. Besides, it's not a good idea to swim right after eating."

"Oh, yeah. Right. Um . . . want to see some outtakes from my last movie?"

I folded my arms. "Are you stalling?"

He smiled. "Yeah!"

"Are you afraid of the water?"

He quickly shook his head. "Nah. Just afraid of looking stupid. I grew up in the Midwest. Landlocked. We were way out in the boonies. No pools. No lakes. I just never learned how to swim. And I've never had the time or the opportunity since then to learn."

"Well, don't worry. Swimming is a cinch. You're a natural athlete. I'll have you swimming in five easy lessons."

"You think?"

"I know!"

"Paddle . . . paddle . . . *paddle!*" I shouted.

"I'm paddling, Mary-Kate!" Nathan gasped. Then he disappeared under the surface.

We were still in the shallow end, so he immediately put his feet down and stood up. He flung his hair back. "What happened? I thought I was paddling."

"Actually, it was more like digging. And you dug yourself down to the bottom. Let's try again."

He tried another couple of times and . . . well . . . sank like a stone. We'd been at it for close to an hour and a half. It was time to break off, so we climbed out of the pool.

Nathan reached for a towel and grabbed his keys off a table so he could drive me to work. "Five easy lessons, huh?"

"Okay. Maybe six." I tried to sound confident, but I'd never seen anybody show less aptitude for swimming than Nathan Richie.

What had Ashley gotten me into?

"Mary-Kate, I need to talk to you." It was Don.

I looked down from my high perch on the lifeguard chair. This was my first time on beach duty. It was a lot harder than working at the pool, and I was exhausted. There was so much more water to watch that I hadn't taken my eyes off the ocean in over an hour. My neck was so stiff, I could hardly move it.

"What's up?" I looked down briefly but then felt my eyes automatically shift back to the water.

"Tonight is the Evening Swim for adults. Can

you stay a little late and work with Dave Lucky on that?"

I puffed my cheeks and blew out a breath. I wanted to spend more time with Dave and try to make up for cutting out on him so many times, but I was too tired to work the extra hours. "Is there anyone else who could do it?" I asked.

Don nodded. "Sure. Kelly or Kareem will be happy to. I just wanted to give you the option of the extra work if you wanted it."

I smiled. "Thanks. I appreciate it. But I think I'll pass on this one."

Don nodded. "No problem. You're doing a great job." He turned away and walked toward the other chair, where Kelly was surveying the waves.

I really did want to spend more time with Dave . . . but I knew I'd have more fun doing it *off* the beach.

"So, did I pass parental inspection?" Greg turned the key in the ignition. "Do I get an official authorized-to-date-Ashley-Olsen card?"

I laughed and buckled my seat belt. "Well, they're not chasing the car to write down your license plate number, so that must mean they like you."

It was our second date. Greg had come over, met my parents, and told them exactly where we were going: Club Sand. Even Mary-Kate looked impressed by that. I knew she and her friends had been trying to get in there for a while.

"I can't believe you have passes for Club Sand. My dad said he's always trying to book bands there. It's the best place for a new group to get attention."

"The club's owner is one of my dad's clients," Greg said, "so he arranged it. I thought we could do some dancing, then have dinner at that new café on the beach. Have you been there?"

I felt a little stab of heartache. "Uh, yes and no. We got there, but it was packed, so we didn't stay."

"Yeah. It's real popular. That's why I made a reservation. Nine-thirty. That okay?"

"Way okay," I answered.

We were sitting in the café, and the place was packed. Even with a reservation we'd had to wait fifteen minutes for a table.

Club Sand had been a total blast. It's a minors' club from five to nine. At nine the minors have to leave and it turns into a regular club with a bar.

We danced until nine, then zipped over to the café to sit and talk.

"So is law interesting?" I asked.

He pretended to yawn.

"It always looks exciting on TV."

"So do breath mints. But when was the last time you got so excited over a mint, you did cartwheels?"

I laughed. "Okay. Okay."

"Must be the same in your business. I mean, planning weddings sounds like fun, but it must be hard work."

"Oh, that is *so* true. You can't imagine how much work goes into one simple event!"

"Yes, I can. My sister got married last year. She turned into a total diva. I mean, you can't believe the stuff she worried about."

"Yes, I can. Because I've got a *real* diva, and she's driving us insane."

He shook his head. "I felt so sorry for the poor guy my sister married. He's totally nice, but I couldn't believe the stuff he had to put up with."

I took a sip of my Mango Frost and looked out over the water. Way in the distance I could see the lights on the graceful yachts moving across the water like fireflies.

I couldn't help sighing. I couldn't imagine a more romantic place to be than out on a yacht in the evening.

"Hello?" Greg waved a hand in front of my eyes.

"Oops. I'm sorry. What were we talking about?"

"Wedding weirdness. I was telling you how difficult my sister was when she was planning hers. And her poor fiancé never said a word."

I took a sip. "Oh, yeah. It must be some kind of prenuptial pattern. Carly and Nathan are exactly like that."

"Does she change her mind about everything— no matter how much trouble it causes?"

He understood! "Big-time!" I said. "We spent days tracking down ten perfectly matched white horses and carriages. Then Carly decided she wanted twelve horses. We tracked those down, and then she decided she wanted *black* horses and open buggies. We found those, and then she decided, never mind, the bridesmaids will ride the horses—*sidesaddle*."

We were laughing hysterically. I could hardly even finish my sentences.

Greg said he was never going to get married; it just made people too weird.

I told him he didn't know how true that was. Talking to Greg was so different from talking to Aaron. I could never have told Aaron half the stuff I told Greg. First of all, Aaron never thought anything I said was funny. Second, he just wasn't that interested in weddings. "Listen, you have to promise me you won't repeat any of this stuff."

"Who would I tell?" He laughed. "My dad? If it's not about tax law, he's not interested. He's probably never even heard of Carly O'Connor and Nathan Richie."

We talked and laughed all the way home. We talked about teachers and television shows and silly stuff we had done. I told him about my Theory of Compatibility and all the craziness it had caused—good and bad.

Greg told me that if I ever needed a good lawyer, I could call his dad. Then he said his dad would probably do it for a very reasonable price. That made us laugh even harder.

Before I knew it, we were kissing good-night on my front step.

It was nice. Not as thrilling as kissing Aaron. But still nice.

I went inside. As I headed upstairs, I realized I hadn't thought about Aaron for hours.

Greg was really good at making me forget Aaron. He was also good at making me forget Ava's pledge. I realized I'd blabbed all kinds of stuff I shouldn't have.

But lawyers had to keep secrets all the time, right?

chapter ten

"**K**ick! Kick! Kick!"

A week later Nathan was still paddling with a Styrofoam board. It was the only way he could keep from sinking.

He kicked from one end of the pool to the other. "Maybe the problem is that I didn't practice between lessons," he confessed. "I'll work on my own before you come back, Mary-Kate. I promise."

"No way! Swimming by yourself is a complete and major no-no. Especially since you *can't* swim."

"I'll stay in the shallow end."

I could feel my chest tighten. "You could still get into trouble. You could faint. You could hit your head. You could have a cramp. A heart attack. An allergic reaction to a bee sting. An electric shock from the lights. Something could fall out of a plane and hit you on the head. You could get attacked by a rabid squirrel. . . ."

Nathan held up his hands. "Okay. Okay! I got it." He gave me a funny look. "That's some imagination you've got there. Ever think about writing disaster movies?"

I smiled. "I've just been thinking about water safety more than usual these days."

"Because . . . ?"

"At work the other day I took my eye off the pool for a second, and a toddler almost fell into the water. Please promise you won't swim alone. If you don't, I won't be able to sleep."

"I wouldn't want you to miss any sleep. I promise to make my motto 'safety first.'" He looked at his watch. "If we don't get going, you'll be late for work."

We got out of the pool. I pulled some shorts on over my suit, grabbed my tote, and followed Nathan to the garage.

Oh, boy! There were five very hot cars in there.

"Which one should we take?" he asked.

Last time he'd had a big SUV waiting out front. If I'd known then what was in the garage . . . I immediately pointed to the red Jag convertible.

"You have good taste. Here!" He tossed me the keys and jumped over the door into the passenger seat. "You drive."

• • •

Talk about a sweet ride. I thought the pink Mustang was cool, but driving a Jaguar convertible is something everybody should do at least once.

I felt like a total movie star. Heads turned to look at me as I wound my way through freeway traffic.

When we neared the beach club, traffic got heavy, so I pulled over and climbed out before the car got boxed in. Nathan scooted over behind the wheel.

I leaned down and peered at him over my sunglasses. "Remember . . ."

"I know! 'Safety first.'" He patted my head and then did a quick U-turn and zoomed away.

I hurried toward the club entrance. Just as I was going in, I saw Dave Lucky. Yea! It had been over a week since the beach party. Between off days and opposite shifts, I hadn't even had a chance to talk to him since that night. I didn't have his phone number and felt weird asking Don for it. Here was my chance to reconnect.

"Mr. Lucky!" I said. "What happened to you at the beach party the other night?"

He was wearing sunglasses, so I couldn't see his eyes. But he didn't smile. "I was beat," he said curtly. He walked through the doorway ahead of me and kept going.

I couldn't believe it. "Lucky Dave" had turned into "Grumpy Dave."

Why? What happened?

❀

"I really appreciate this, Ashley."

"No problem." Saturdays were supposed to be my day off, but Ava had asked me to come in. The bridesmaids' dresses had been delivered that morning. And Saddles 'N' Stirrups was on the way over with the sidesaddles.

"Why don't you get the steamer, and we'll unpack the dresses," Ava suggested. "I'll get out the list of bridesmaids, and we'll make sure everything's here."

A few minutes later Ava opened the first box, and we both gasped.

Carly might be picky and a diva, but she had wonderful taste. The dresses had stiff brocade bodices, the colors the shades of peach and straw you find in antique French tapestries. The skirts were full and made out of yards of watered silk.

One by one we took out the gowns and steamed them, then hung them on racks and spaced them far apart so they wouldn't get wrinkled.

When the doorbell rang, Ava opened the door just a crack. I peered out over her shoulder.

Two men had several huge boxes stacked on dollies. "Weddings by Ava?"

"That's right." Ava slipped out the door so the deliverymen couldn't see inside. She signed for the packages.

"Want us to carry them inside?" one of the men asked.

"No, thank you," Ava said. "We'll do it."

"They're heavy."

Ava smiled. "We'll be fine."

"Okay by me. It's your back."

"Argh!" We dropped the last heavy box in the middle of the room and flopped down into our chairs.

"I thought sidesaddles were small," I wailed. "These must weigh a ton apiece."

Ava mopped her forehead. "Let's see what they look like."

We pried open one of the boxes and lifted out a sidesaddle. It must have been one of those ancient Scottish warrior queen sidesaddles. I had never seen so many silver doodads, leather tassels, and fancy tooling in my life.

"What are the bridesmaids going to say when they see these things?" I asked.

Ava began to laugh. "I have no idea. I got an e-mail from Carly this morning. She said she's going to give the saddles to her bridesmaids as brides-maids' gifts instead of bracelets."

85

We laughed hysterically. "I'm sure they're just what they've always wanted," I said. "So much more useful than a beautiful bracelet."

It took us two hours, but we unpacked all the saddles and hauled the empty boxes out to the curb.

"Now what?" I asked.

Ava smiled. "Now you get to put on a dress and make sure you can actually sit on one of these while wearing it."

Great! I wanted to try one on so badly, but I was too afraid to even ask.

Lenore's dress fit me perfectly. When I came out of the dressing room, Ava clapped her hands to her cheeks. "Those dresses cost a fortune, but they're worth every penny. Look at you. You're gorgeous!"

I looked at myself in the full-length mirror. "I feel like a princess."

Ava heaved one of the saddles over a stool. "Okay, Cinderella. Take a test drive."

I sat on the saddle. It felt like making a parachute landing. All that silk poufed out in every direction. It covered the entire saddle *and* the stool. If I'd been on an actual horse, it probably would have covered its head and tail, too.

Ava realized this as well and shook her head. "Not good. See if you can get the alterations lady lined up for next week. We're going to have to pull some material out of those skirts."

"I guess ancient Scottish warrior queens didn't wear bridesmaid dresses on horseback," I said.

The phone rang. Ava picked it up. "Weddings by Ava. . . . Yes . . . Oh! Great. I'll be there in twenty minutes." She hung up. "The caterer wants to show me some more table settings. A messenger is supposed to deliver some candle samples. Would you mind the store until he comes? Then you can lock up and leave."

"No problem." I bounced on the saddle as if I were riding. Suddenly I slid off backward, and the huge skirt covered me completely! "Yeow!"

"Ashley! Are you all right?"

I could hear Ava. But I couldn't see her. I fought my way out from under the silk pouf and managed to sit up.

Ava laughed and pulled me to my feet. "Make a note in the style guide to add a layer of textured voile over the silk. It'll grip the seat of the saddle."

While I was marveling at her knowledge of everything fabric, she headed out. I did some stuff at the computer and answered some e-mails. I was still wearing the dress. I don't know why. It was just fun to wear. I kept twirling and sort of dancing around.

There was a knock on the door.

Ah! The messenger. He was going to think this was a mighty fancy office when I opened the door.

"Good day," I said in a silly "princess" voice as I opened the door.

But it wasn't a messenger. It was Greg.

"Hey! Hi! Whoa! What is *that*? A costume or something?" Greg's mouth fell open. "Wait a minute. I know what that is. It's Carly's wedding dress, isn't it?"

I realized I had made a terrible mistake by opening the door wearing the dress. It was a good thing it was only Greg. If it had been a reporter with a camera, the tabloids would have exactly the kind of photo op we didn't want them to have.

I ducked behind the door and just stuck my head out. "No, it's not."

He chuckled. "Yes, it is! But why are *you* wearing it?"

"It's a bridesmaid's dress."

"Wow! You're one of the bridesmaids?"

"I *wish*! No. We're just making sure they work."

"Work?" That confused him, and he shook his head to clear it.

"Don't ask," I begged.

He smiled. "Okay. I won't. Listen, I called your house, and your mom said you were here." He produced a picnic basket from behind his back. "I wanted to see if you were up for lunch in the park."

Talk about cute. It was a real old-fashioned picnic basket. "I have sandwiches. I have veggies. I have sodas. I have cookies. I have everything except someone to eat it with."

"I wish I could. But I'm waiting for a messenger."

"When is he coming?"

"I don't know. That's why I'm hanging around."

"Maybe we could just have the picnic here."

I sighed. Nobody was supposed to come into Ava's until after the wedding. Not even Mary-Kate. Ava had been totally clear on that.

"Ashley?" He waved a hand in front of my face.

"Sorry. I was just trying to figure out what to do about this."

"Are you still worried that I might be a spy?" He grinned.

"No. But I want to respect Ava's rules."

He nodded easily. "Then how about we eat in the front yard?"

The "front yard" was a tiny patch of ground cover with some flagstone steps. Still, it would have worked if there hadn't been a huge clap of thunder, and rain hadn't started pouring down.

Greg took a few steps closer to the door so he could stand underneath the roof of the little front porch. "Well, I guess that's it for our picnic. I'll just wait for this to stop, and then I'll leave."

I felt awful. After all his trouble, I was making him huddle under a tiny roof while rain slipped down the back of his collar. "I'm sorry," I told him. "I really am."

"No problem. But here. Take the food." He opened the picnic basket. I saw two pretty plates, two forks, and checkered cloth napkins. He'd really gone all out.

This was ridiculous. I couldn't believe I was acting so stupid. "I'm being an idiot. Come inside."

"You sure? I don't want you to get into trouble."

"Ava trusts me, and I trust you. Come on in."

I opened the door, and he came in. When he saw the dresses hanging in a row and the sidesaddles on the backs of all the furniture, he laughed. "Whoa! I thought you were joking about the sidesaddles."

"Let me change. I'll be right back."

"I'll set up the lunch." He headed into the kitchenette.

I went into the bedroom that we used as a changing room and put my own clothes back on. When I came back out, Greg was sipping a soda and looking at all the sketches pinned up on the walls.

"These look like sets and costumes for a movie," he said. "Is it all for the wedding?"

"Yes. It's going to be the most incredible wedding ever."

"Wow. What's that?" He pointed to a picture of the California Historical Winery. "It looks like a castle."

"It's one of the oldest wineries in California. The original building dates back to 1754. You'd have to see the inside to believe it. It's gorgeous. Exactly like an old European castle."

"And that's where they're having the wedding?"

"Yes. Carly loved it."

He whistled. "This must be costing a fortune."

"Totally. But Carly and Nathan said money was no object. They want what they want."

"Well, I know what I want. I want a sandwich," he said. "Are you hungry?"

"Starving." I laughed, and then I used a fake "royalty" voice. "Riding always gives me an appetite!"

chapter eleven

I was in the break room. We'd closed the beach and cleared the pool because of the rain. Most people had left, and Don told us we lifeguards could leave, too, since the weather wasn't expected to change.

Lucky Dave came over to me. "Mary-Kate, have you seen Kareem?"

So now he was speaking to me again? I'd tried to talk to him three times this morning. He blew me off every time.

"No," I said curtly. I really didn't appreciate being jerked around. Why pretend I wasn't annoyed?

But when he started to walk away, I wanted to kick myself.

What was I doing? If he was finally trying to talk to me, I should try to talk back. Something had happened to get us off track, and I really wanted to know what it was. "Hey, Lucky Dave," I called out.

"Don't you mean, 'Hey, Stupid'?" he answered in an angry tone.

"What does *that* mean?"

"It means I actually thought you were interested in me. That makes me 'Stupid Dave.'"

What was he talking about? "Why would that make you stupid?"

"I finally got it. I finally understand why every time we're together, you're constantly looking around at other people and running off. I know your dad's in the music business. And I know you're friends with Danielle Bloom. But I *finally* got it when I saw you with Nathan Richie."

What did he get? "I still don't know what you're talking about."

"You're a celebrity snob. One of those people who's always looking around to see if there's somebody cooler to hang with. I'm sorry I'm not a movie star. I'm just plain old Dave Lucky. So quit acting like you're interested in being with me and then dropping me the second you see somebody more fascinating."

I sucked in my breath in a gasp. I wanted to scream, *"You really* are *stupid! I'm just giving Nathan Richie swimming lessons, you idiot!"*

But I couldn't reveal anything about Ava's

clients, or I'd get Ashley into some serious trouble.

"That's totally not true," I said, trying to defend myself.

"Then tell me what's going on. Why are you avoiding me?"

I opened and closed my mouth. I couldn't tell the truth, but I didn't want to lie because: A) It's wrong, and B) I couldn't think one up fast enough. But I knew I had to say something.

"I swear I wasn't avoiding you. I'm so sorry for being distracted or disappearing. I can explain. I'm good friends with Danielle. I just went over to say hi that night and I got caught up in her water fight, and—"

For a moment Dave looked a bit embarrassed, like he'd made a big deal out of nothing. He even looked kind of shy as he asked, "So what about Nathan Richie? How do you know him? He's a famous movie star."

Uh-oh. Why had I picked the red Jag for a ride? "We're not friends exactly, but . . ."

Dave gave me a skeptical look. "So what are you then?"

"I . . . I really can't tell you. I promised."

Dave's expression hardened into the look he'd given me earlier. "Yeah. Sure. Whatever. See ya 'round," he snapped.

Then he walked off.

94

• • •

I called Ashley to pick me up, but she was still at her office, waiting for a messenger. So I got a ride to Click Café from Kelly.

I figured I'd kill the afternoon at the coffee bar and listen to the rain pound on the roof. It made a nice, glum sound to go with my nice, glum mood.

Brittany and Lauren were sitting at the counter talking to Malcolm, who was leaning against a wall pretending to listen to them while he read a computer magazine.

Brittany gave me a big smile. "Hi, Mary-Kate. Did you wash out today?"

"Big time," I said. She had no idea. I ordered an espresso and tried not to look as gloomy as I felt.

Lauren smiled. "So what do you think about Ashley's new guy?"

"He seems nice enough."

Behind his magazine Malcolm raised one eyebrow. "Ooh, faint praise."

"I didn't mean it that way," I said. But the second I said I didn't mean it that way, I realized I *did* mean it that way.

Ashley seemed to like Greg Johnson a lot. But to me it looked like what she liked was that he was so organized compared to Aaron. I didn't understand why she was into Greg romantically. He wasn't like most of the guys she dated.

I'd only met him once, briefly, so I couldn't quite put my finger on what felt wrong about him. There was something just too conveniently perfect about Greg Johnson.

chapter twelve

"**H**e thinks you're a celebrity snob?" Ashley was stunned.

"Yeah! Can you believe that?"

We were sitting in Ashley's room that night and I was telling her about my run-in with Lucky Dave.

"So what did you tell him?"

"What *could* I tell him? That I'm teaching Nathan Richie how to swim? I couldn't. So I just said that it wasn't what he thought. The ultimate lame-o comeback."

Ashley plopped down into the big beanbag chair. "Oh, boy!"

"Oh, boy is right." I chewed a cuticle. "Because I actually am *not* teaching Nathan Richie how to swim. He's making no progress at all."

"*Mary-Kate!*" Ashley wailed. "I'm counting on you."

"I'm doing my best! But Nathan Richie was just not born to swim. They say muscle weighs more than fat. He's all muscle. Maybe that's why he keeps sinking."

I got up and paced around. "Listen, I'm not really a swimming instructor. I just figured he was such a natural athlete, he'd pick it up. But I think he needs a real instructor."

"But he won't get one. He says he can't trust anyone he hires not to talk to reporters! You can't give up!" Ashley wailed. "Please promise me you'll teach him to swim. If he can't swim, Carly will find out that he lied. And she might just pull out of the wedding!"

"Wouldn't that be kind of drastic?"

"Of course!"

"Would she do something like that?"

"She might!"

I sighed. "Okay. I'll keep working on it."

Ashley smiled. "Great. Because I'd hate to have to send back all those sidesaddles."

"Sidesaddles?"

Ashley slapped a hand over her mouth.

"What sidesaddles?" I asked.

"I can't tell you," she said through her fingers.

I rolled my eyes.

"Please don't do that. You're making me feel just like Greg did."

"Huh?"

Ashley told me how Greg had come to Ava's with a totally romantic picnic lunch. She also told me they'd wound up eating there because of the rain.

"Hold it! Are you telling me you won't let your own *sister* into Ava's, but you let Greg in? Wow, Ashley, you must like this guy a lot."

"What's not to like?" she asked with a smile.

"I know he's cute. And you said he really pays attention. But, I don't know. . . . It's all so fast after Aaron. How well do you really know him?"

Ashley shrugged. "All I know is that Greg is a great guy, and I can really talk to him."

She used to say that about Aaron. Now I definitely had a funny feeling about this.

❀

When the doorbell rang after dinner, I thought it was Lauren coming over to watch DVDs with Mary-Kate and me. But it was Greg.

I smiled. "Hi! What are you doing here?"

He gave me a quick hug and a kiss. "I am really sorry, Ashley."

"About what?"

"My mom called. She fell and broke her leg. I've got to go home."

I could feel my face fall. "You're going back to New York?" I heard Mary-Kate come down the stairs behind me.

"Only for a couple of weeks, until she gets her walking cast. I need to help with shopping, housekeeping, getting the dogs walked—all that stuff. Mainly she can't be alone right now."

I understood completely. But it was still kind of a shock.

His car was at the curb. "I'm going to the airport now. I'll call you in a couple of days," he promised. "I'll be back in, like, two weeks."

He kissed me again. But it was a distracted kiss. He was definitely in a hurry to leave. Probably because he was worried about his mom.

I watched his taillights disappear down the block. When he turned the corner, I realized I didn't have his number in New York.

❀

"Stroke! Turn! Breathe! Stroke! Turn! Breathe!"

Nathan's form was excellent. His head turned with rhythmic precision. His breathing was even and deep.

I clapped my hands. "That's great! Now let's try it in the water."

Nathan stopped churning his arms. "Do we have to, Mary-Kate?" He pretended to whine, but his eyes were twinkling. "I mean, everything is going so well *here* by the side of the pool."

I'd finally suggested that we work outside the pool so Nathan could get a feel for the timing.

100

In the water he seemed to be able to kick his legs and stroke with his arms at the same time. But he couldn't quite coordinate turning his head to the side and breathing. That meant he could only "swim" as long as he could hold his breath. Which was something. At least now he wasn't sinking.

We jumped into the water. I grabbed the Styrofoam board. "Here. Put this under your chest. It'll help keep you on top of the water while you practice."

Nathan took the board and began to wriggle it under his chest. The board was buoyant, and the harder he pushed it under the water, the more resistance it gave.

Finally, it slipped out of his hands.

POP! The board shot straight up out of the water . . . and . . .

"Ouch!"

. . . it hit Nathan right in the mouth.

"So you're sure it's okay for you to swim?" I asked Nathan the next day.

"Of course," he said. "I only knocked out a crown. It wasn't a big deal—except that spending all day at the dentist isn't exactly my idea of fun."

Yesterday had been a total loss after Nathan got popped in the mouth. He had to be more careful.

Nathan was a very handsome guy. People paid a lot of money to look at his face!

"Do you have a mouth guard?" I asked.

"Yeah. I wear it when I box."

"Maybe you should wear it while you swim."

I was joking, but he took me seriously.

"That's not a bad idea. I'll go get it."

I tried not to laugh. As an action-adventure star, I guess he took safety seriously.

He ran into the house and was back in minutes, wearing his mouth guard. "Okay," he said in a muffled voice. "What now?"

Since the breathing work would be tougher with the mouth guard in, I decided to keep his face out of the water, for now. "Let's work on the backstroke."

I put one hand under his back to guide him. "Okay. Now kick and stroke. Kick and stroke."

Nathan started moving his arms and legs. "Great. Great. Great!" I watched his legs. They were moving in perfect rhythm with his arms. "Keep it up! That's great. A little faster now. One, two. One, two. One, two." We were moving from one side of the shallow end to the other. "One, two. One, two. One . . ."

I was so busy watching his legs, I forgot to watch his arms, and . . .

"*Ouch!*"

. . . he backstroked right into the wall, banging his head and his hand on the concrete deck.

"It doesn't hurt," he insisted.

"But it's swelling."

He tightened the cold pack around his wrist and pressed the ice bag against his head. "This will take care of it."

"I think you should see a doctor."

"Absolutely not." He opened the kitchen door and shooed me toward the garage.

"But—"

"Look, I get injured a lot on film sets. Trust me. I'll be fine. Here. You drive." He winced as he reached into his pocket for keys.

This time he didn't toss them. He couldn't. His wrist was too sore.

I leaned over and took them. We got into the car, and I backed it out of the garage. In the harsh glare of the sunlight Nathan didn't look so good.

Nathan didn't need just a mouth guard. To work with me, America's Number One Box Office Action-Adventure Hero needed a bicycle helmet, a life jacket, and maybe a protective layer of bubble wrap.

❀

"Hey, Ash, since when don't you like pineapple?"

Brittany pointed to my fruit salad, most of which was still on my plate.

"I'm just not hungry," I said.

Brittany and Lauren looked at each other. "Not hungry because of Aaron? Or not hungry because of Greg?"

I picked up my fork and poked at a strawberry. "Probably a little of both," I said.

"Have you heard from Greg?"

I shook my head. "No. I tried to call his cell, but it wasn't on or something."

"Have you heard from Aaron?"

I squinted and pretended to be mad. "You are the nosiest friends I have ever had."

Lauren cocked her head. "We're your friends. That's our job. It's what we do."

Actually I was grateful for them. I was feeling pretty alone these days. No Aaron. No Greg.

I looked at my watch. It was time to get back to my job. I crossed my fingers that Mary-Kate was making progress with Nathan. At least something good might be happening. . . .

"No! Not the green napkins, the *gold* ones. Well, I'm sorry you don't have the gold ones in stock. You'll have to order them."

Ava was on the phone. Things were frantic. Carly was going to be back from Europe any day now. We weren't sure just when, but we wanted to have everything ready when she arrived.

104

"Then charter a plane and fly them in from Hong Kong," Ava finally sputtered. "I don't care what it costs." She slammed down the phone and reached for her aspirin bottle. "I am so worried!" She rifled through piles of stuff on her desk.

"About the napkins?"

"No. I lost something."

"What?"

"Their style guide. It was in a big envelope and it had *style guide* scribbled on the flap."

I felt my stomach turn over. The style guide had our notes on everything from the dresses to the invitations. It was the blueprint for the entire wedding.

"Do you remember seeing it anywhere?" She sounded a little desperate.

I could see it clearly in my head. It was on top of Ava's desk. But that had been days ago.

She opened a drawer and looked through it. "Do you think it's possible it got sent out somewhere by mistake?"

My heart began to thump uncomfortably.

I had mailed or messengered at least three hundred packages and envelopes over the last week. Had I sent that envelope to one of the gazillions of vendors, florists, caterers, hoteliers, or wedding party members by accident?

I felt my face flush hot. Ava had hired me

because I was detail-oriented. This kind of mistake was unforgivable.

Ava snapped her fingers. "Wait a minute! I know where it is." She placed a hand over her forehead. "I took a briefcase full of work home with me yesterday. A lot of stuff is still in my study. I'm sure it's there."

I was so relieved, my legs felt wobbly. Just as I was congratulating myself on not messing things up, the door flew open with a huge *CRASH*, and Carly stormed into Weddings by Ava.

chapter thirteen

Ava and I both jumped up.

"Carly!" Ava gasped. "Are you—" She was clearly going to say, "Are you *nuts*?" But she broke off and corrected herself just in time. "Are you *back*?"

Carly put her hands on her hips. Her hair was so short it stood up all over. She wore some kind of rubber zip-up jacket with matching pants and thigh-high boots over the pants.

It was as if we were under attack by the Supermodel from Outer Space.

"I *am* back. And I have two things to say to you. Number one: The wedding as planned is cancelled. Number two: You're *fired!* I'm hiring somebody else and starting over."

Ava and I looked at each other, looked at the door, which was sort of hanging from the frame, and then took a step back. Carly was clearly crazed about something. We didn't know whether she was in commando character or just being herself. Either way we felt safer with a little distance between us and her.

Ava spoke first. "What's this all about, Carly? Have we done something to upset you?"

Carly held out a newspaper. "Read this."

Ava took it. I stood next to her so I could see. It was the front page of *Celebrity View*. It promised a *Sneak Peek* at the *Top Secret Wedding Plans of Carly O'Connor and Nathan Richie*.

Ava gasped. She opened the paper, and there it was: a full-color, two-page spread featuring pictures of the dresses, the sidesaddles, the floral arrangements, and the old stone winery where Carly and Nathan were planning to marry.

Everything was reported down to the last detail . . . *by Greg Johnson*.

No mistake. It was the same Greg Johnson. There was even a little picture of him and a short bio. *Greg Johnson is a senior at Holbrook High and a summer intern for* Celebrity View.

So Greg Johnson wasn't really a summer intern for his father's law firm. He was a summer snoop for a newspaper.

My heart pounded in my chest. He'd totally fooled me. Totally used me. He'd probably seen me going in and out of Ava's for days and then waited for me at Ooh La Latte Café. How could I have been so stupid? How? *How?*

I was shaking all over. I'd ruined everything—Carly's wedding *and* Ava's business.

"How could this happen?" Carly shouted.

Ava shook her head. "I am so sorry. It's all my fault."

Her fault? What was Ava talking about?

"I took your style guide home and apparently I lost it. I guess whoever found it sold it to the paper. I take full responsibility."

For one split second I almost considered letting Ava go on thinking that.

But I couldn't. I couldn't let somebody else take the blame for something I did. "It wasn't your fault," I managed to croak.

"Yes, it is," Ava insisted. "It's the only explanation. There hasn't been one person in this office except for you, me, Carly, and Nathan."

"There was . . . someone else," I said. My voice sounded high and thin. "Greg Johnson is a friend of mine—*was* a friend," I quickly corrected. "I didn't know he worked for a newspaper. He was here last week. I guess he took . . . the style guide."

I never saw anybody look as devastated as Ava. It was horrible.

"It was all my fault," I said to Carly. "And I am so, *so* sorry."

Carly kicked one of the sidesaddles off a chair. "I don't care whose fault it is. It shouldn't have happened." She turned around and marched out. "Send my agent a bill for your door," she spat over one shoulder.

Ava sat down and stared at me, biting her lower lip. I waited, dreading what was coming.

She was so angry, her voice shook. But she didn't shout. She kept her voice low—which was somehow worse than shouting. "Ashley, I have rules for a reason. I explained the reasons to you. You indicated to me that you understood those reasons. Clearly you don't have the judgment or the maturity this job requires. I'm letting you go. As of right now."

I hung my head. "I'm sorry."

Ava shrugged. "I know this sounds harsh, but I don't care if you're sorry. The damage is done. All the apologies in the world won't fix it."

I picked up my purse and jacket and left. I'd never felt so awful in my life.

I've made some pretty big mistakes before, but nothing as huge as this one. My parents were going to be so disappointed. And who could blame them?

The only good thing I could see coming out of this was that Nathan would learn to swim and . . .

Oh, no! Carly's next stop was bound to be

Nathan's house. Mary-Kate was supposed to be there right now. She needed to get out of there— *fast*.

I grabbed my phone and started frantically dialing. *Pick up, Mary-Kate! Pick up! Red alert! Red alert! Incoming!*

But there was no answer.

❀

My mom had just dropped me off at Nathan's, and I could hear the phone in the house ringing when he opened the door.

I stepped inside. "Do you need to get that?"

He shook his head. "Let it ring. I don't want to talk to anybody right now."

He was wearing a pair of khaki shorts, not a bathing suit.

"Is something wrong?"

He ran a hand through his hair. "I read through the script again last night. There is just no way I can do what I'm supposed to do in this movie."

"You're giving up?"

He rolled his eyes. "I am not a swimmer. I need to tell my agent to pull me out, then figure out something to tell Carly."

He turned and started walking through the empty house. I hurried behind him, trying to keep up. "But . . . but . . ."

He was upset. And because he was upset, he

was mad. "I am the number one action-adventure hero in the business! I want to *stay* the number one action-adventure hero in the business. But I will *not* be the number one action-adventure hero in the business if I *drown!*"

"You're giving up too soon. You're getting better every day. Just a few more lessons and you're there!"

He came to a stop. I ran into him and bounced off. *Ouch!* The man was a wall of muscles.

"Sorry," he said. "Look, Mary-Kate, I really appreciate your help but—"

The phone started ringing again. He picked it up and slammed it down. "Probably the director," he said. "I've been ducking his calls for a week."

❀

"Ow!" I yanked the phone away from my ear. It sounded as if somebody had slammed the receiver down.

Mary-Kate's cell wasn't on. I'd been redialing Nathan's house like mad, trying to get somebody to pick up. But what was that phone smackdown all about? It couldn't be a sign of anything good.

I started running toward the car. I needed to get to Nathan Richie's place fast.

Hurricane Carly was about to hit.

I'd gotten my sister into this. I needed to get her out before she got blown away.

❀

"So you're just giving up?" I followed Nathan into the kitchen, where he grabbed a bottle of water out of the refrigerator.

"That's right. It's just too big a risk. It could damage my career."

Now *I* was mad. "Some action-adventure hero you are!"

He narrowed his eyes. "That was low."

I put my hands on my hips. "You know what you are? You're *chicken!*"

"Cut it out." He stalked out the kitchen door to the backyard.

I followed him. "I'm serious. You're not afraid of drowning. You're not afraid of damaging your career. You're just afraid of looking stupid. You're afraid people might laugh at you." I couldn't believe I was talking to a big Hollywood star this way, but I couldn't stop. I had to tell him what I thought.

His face turned grim. "Not *people*," he growled. "*One* person. Carly."

"But she loves you," I said.

"She loves Nathan Richie. Nathan Richie, the action-adventure hero. *Not* Nathan Richie, just some dork who can't even swim."

"You must think she's really shallow."

"No, she's not. But she *lives* her work. I love that. I love that she's so intense. That she's passionate. That she demands a lot from herself and from other people. You wouldn't understand."

That did it. "I wouldn't understand?" I said. "I understand that you love Carly, and you want to make her happy. And she loves you, which is why she wants this wedding to be perfect. Why do you think Ashley risked her job to get you a swim coach? Because we all know how much Carly wants to marry you."

He pushed his hair out of his eyes. "I didn't think about that."

"We *all* have a lot at stake here. So *please* . . . just give it one more try. You know how much this will mean to Carly."

I could tell I'd hit a nerve.

"Alright. Let's do it."

I kicked off my shoes and followed him into the pool, still in my clothes. "Remember. Kick. Stroke. Breathe. Take it slowly, and don't think so much."

Nathan slowly put his head down and then let the length of his body slide along the surface of the water.

He started with his arms first, forgetting his legs. His lower torso began to sink. He flexed his body like a dolphin to correct his position, then remembered to kick.

His powerful strokes and kicks began to propel him forward.

Breathe! I thought. *Breathe!* Come on, Nathan . . . *breathe*!

It seemed as if my brain waves finally got through to him. He turned his head, and I heard him breathe in.

All right!

He did it again . . . and again. He reached the other end of the pool—the deep end. Could he handle it? Or would he panic?

I held my breath, poised to swim to the rescue. But he didn't choke and go under. He turned around and came swimming back.

The man wasn't just swimming. He was swimming laps!

I started jumping up and down. "You're swimming!" I screamed. "Nathan, you're doing it!"

He came back to the shallow end, put his feet down, and shot up out of the water with a wild whoop! And he completely splashed me.

I laughed as I wiped water out of my eyes, but I couldn't believe what I saw when I opened them.

Carly! She was standing by the pool with her arms folded over her chest. And she was soaking wet.

Water dripped from her short hair down the collar of her jacket and into her thigh-high designer boots.

I backed up a little. Carly O'Connor was famous for her temper.

But she didn't look angry. She was smiling. In fact, she was beaming. "Darling," she said, staring at Nathan. "You learned to swim! I am so proud of you!"

Nathan's mouth fell open. Then he rubbed his hands over his face. "You *knew*? You *knew* I couldn't swim?"

"Of course I knew," Carly said. "Your agent told my agent that you were trying to get the script changed. The only real difference was where the action took place, so I figured it out. I was just waiting for you to tell me yourself."

"Then . . . you're not mad?"

"Well, I'm sorry that you didn't trust me with the truth. But I'm impressed that you've learned to swim so quickly. You looked amazing just now!" Her eyes were shining, and the grin on Nathan's face was proof that they were going to work it all out.

She finally took a good look at me. She pointed a finger and shook her head. "Aren't you . . . ?"

"I'm Mary-Kate Olsen," I said. "Ashley's sister. We look a lot alike."

Carly's smile disappeared. If her face had been a door, it would have shut with a *bang*. "Then you can march right out of here," she said.

"Carly, what's wrong?" Nathan asked.

"What's wrong is that Ashley Olsen and Ava

totally betrayed our trust. I never want to hear from or see either one of them again."

That's when Ashley came running out into the yard. "Mary-Kate! Mary-Kate!" Ashley cried. "You need to leave fast! Carly is coming. And she is *mad!*"

Talk about bad timing.

chapter fourteen

O*ops!* I saw Carly and skidded to a stop. Oh, no! She'd beaten me here. I looked at Mary-Kate and Nathan. Everybody seemed okay.

But then Carly's eyes narrowed. She pointed to the door. "Out!" she yelled. "Both of you! Out!"

Mary-Kate hopped out of the pool, jumped into her Skecher mules, and ran to my side.

"We're going," I said quickly. "We're going!"

"Hold it!" Nathan jumped out of the pool. "Carly! What's going on? What are you talking about?"

She pointed to me. "This girl sold Ava's style guide to our wedding to *Celebrity View.*"

"That's not *true!*" I cried. "The style guide was *stolen!* It was stolen by a guy who was just pretending to like me so he could get information about your wedding."

Mary-Kate's eyes got huge. "What? When did this happen?"

"I just found out." I handed Mary-Kate the newspaper.

Mary-Kate let out a shriek. "That jerk!"

"Is this the guy who broke up with you?" Nathan asked me.

I shook my head. "No. This is another guy."

Nathan put an arm around my shoulder. "Wow, I'm sorry. That must hurt."

"I was stupid and I ruined your wedding. I am really, really sorry," I turned to Carly. "He tricked me into letting him into Ava's and he stole the style guide. I know my being sorry doesn't change my being stupid. But I don't want you to think I did it on purpose. Or for money. Or—"

"It's okay, Ashley. I think you've been through enough," Nathan said.

I felt relieved knowing that at least Nathan wasn't upset with me. But Carly didn't look any happier.

"'It's okay'? Our whole wedding is ruined! How is that okay?" Carly asked him. She didn't look like a mega movie star to me anymore. She looked like an unhappy young woman on the verge of tears.

Nathan took Carly's hand. "Of course it's okay. So we have to figure out something besides sidesaddles for your bridesmaids. We've already changed our minds a few times—what's one more? And besides, I kinda owe Ashley. If it wasn't for her, I wouldn't have learned how to swim."

Carly looked stubborn. "I'm sorry, Nathan, but I still don't trust her."

I felt my heart sink again. Nathan might be a tough guy on the screen, but this seemed like a more difficult situation than any disaster movie. I didn't think anything would change Carly's mind about me or Ava.

"Look, Ashley admitted that what she did was stupid. But you forgave *me* for not telling you the truth. We all mess up," Nathan argued.

"But, Nathan, I love you, and I trust you! And think of all the money and time we've already put into this wedding. Now we have to start all over again just to get the press off the story!"

"Carly," Nathan said, "I know how much this wedding means to you, because it means the same thing to me. And I know how much work you've put into it. But trust me. It'll be perfect no matter where we are or what we're wearing or how the bridesmaids and groomsmen get down the aisle, because I still get to be married to you at the end of the ceremony."

Wow! Way to go Nathan!

Carly gave him a long look. Then her face softened and she smiled. "You're right. I can't wait to be married to you. I guess we can let Ashley off the hook."

He wrapped his arms around her and started to pull her in for a kiss, but Carly laughed as she put her hands on his chest and pushed him backward into the pool.

He came up laughing and then pulled her in after him, designer boots and all.

The next thing I knew, they were laughing and wrestling and splashing and basically having a ball.

"Hey! No horseplay!" Mary-Kate yelled, pretending to be a lifeguard.

They answered her with a tidal wave of a splash that soaked us both.

❀

"Hey, Lucky Dave!"

Dave Lucky was walking down the street toward the club. He did a double take when he saw me sitting in the back of Nathan's Jag.

Nathan was driving, and Carly sat in the passenger seat with an arm draped over his shoulders. I had checked with Don to see when Dave was working again. They had brought me to work this morning just about when I figured Dave would show up. We'd hung out in the parking lot—away from the main street in case reporters spotted the Jag—until I saw him walking toward the club. I gave Nathan his cue, and we cruised along at the same speed Lucky Dave was walking. Nathan did the talking.

"Dave," he said in a man-to-man voice, "we need to talk. Mary-Kate tells me you got a wrong impression somehow. So Carly and I came along to clear things up." Dave's eyes went from Nathan to Carly to me and back to Carly. He was clearly stunned to have Nathan Richie talking to him.

Nathan stopped the car, and I got out.

"I couldn't tell you before because it was a secret," I began. "But I've been helping Nathan block out some swimming stunts for his next movie."

Dave's eyebrows shot up. "Really?"

I caught a faint wink from Nathan. It wasn't *exactly* the truth, but it was close enough.

"It was a secret because Mary-Kate's sister is helping with our wedding," Carly explained in her sweetest voice. "We didn't want reporters hounding Mary-Kate for information, too." She bestowed her full-on movie-star smile on Dave. I think he started to blush. Could this be working?

"Remember, Mary-Kate," Nathan added, "we start the advanced work next week. See you then." Nathan and Carly waved and drove off. It was just Dave and me now, face to face in the sun.

"No wonder you're always avoiding me. You're not just a great lifeguard, you're an amazing secret-keeper. That's incredible!" He reached for my hand, but I pulled away. I had to get this straight right now.

"And you're not just an idiot, you're a stupid idiot. I never avoided you."

"Yes, you did. Every time I tried to talk to you, you either ran off or refused to look at me."

I groaned. *Oh no! Talk about a misunderstanding!* "Dave, I'm so sorry! I swear I wasn't running off or refusing to look at you. I think I got a little too carried away with the lifeguard thing," I explained. "I just couldn't take my eyes off the water. Even when we were at the beach party."

I told him about the toddler at the edge of the pool. I even told him that the reason I hadn't been watching the water was that I was on the lookout for *him*.

That made him smile, and his eyes twinkled even as he nodded in understanding. "That's pretty scary. I'm glad the kid's okay." He reached for my hand again, and I let him take it. "Now that we have all that straightened out, do you think we could go out sometime?"

I smiled. "Well, now that you mention it, I'm pretty sure I'm going to need a date for this wedding that's coming up."

chapter fifteen

"**I** am *so* glad you talked her out of that side-saddle thing!" Carly's sister said. The more I got to know Lenore, the more I liked her. She was awesome. Every bit as pretty as Carly and totally down to earth.

Ava winked at me. "We didn't exactly 'talk her out of it.' Carly's pretty strong-minded. She just decided to go in another direction."

We were leaning against a polished brass rail looking out at the gorgeous ocean.

In honor of Nathan's newly acquired skill, Carly had decided to go with an aquatic theme.

"Tell me about this yacht," Lenore said. "It's fabulous!"

"Supposedly it once belonged to a pirate," Ava explained. "Now it's a floating palace."

Lenore grinned. "Which means it was perfect for Carly. How did you find it?"

Ava put a hand on my shoulder. "My trusty assistant found it."

I felt great. I had really earned Ava's trust back. We had both worked day and night. But the hardest part had been finding the right new location for the wedding.

My date with Greg had given me the idea of an evening wedding on the water. But I couldn't figure out how to make it happen. Finally, after hours of phone calls and a Net search, I'd found the perfect setting.

"This yacht has a really interesting history," I told Lenore. "It was almost taken apart for scrap materials about forty years ago. But one of the movie studios bought it for a set. After that it sat in storage until it was auctioned off two years ago. A European company bought it and restored it to use and lease out as a small luxury cruise ship."

Lenore smiled. "Well, you guys did a fabulous job!" She thanked us again and then went off to talk to some other guests.

Ava and I lifted our glasses of sparkling water and toasted each other. "I can't believe we're really crossing the finish line," said Ava. "I never could have done it without you, Ashley. Thank you for all your hard work."

"Thank you for giving me a second—I mean, *third*—chance," I answered.

She patted my shoulder. "They say the third time's the charm. And aren't we a great team? I don't think any two wedding planners could have done a better job."

Everything was running like clockwork. The guests were being ferried to the yacht in a small armada of glass-bottomed boats. Around and under the boats a hundred swimmers in mermaid costumes performed water ballets right out of an old movie.

Stewards in white jackets circulated along the shining wooden deck of the yacht. They welcomed guests aboard with glasses of champagne and sparkling water.

Mary-Kate and Lucky Dave came over to stand next to us. "Wow." Mary-Kate sighed. "I think every movie star and celebrity in Hollywood is on this yacht."

"And no reporters!" I added.

When the last guest was aboard, as the sun was setting, the ship's captain asked for everyone's attention. The wedding was about to begin.

The cabin doors opened. The orchestra struck up the bridal march, and Carly and Nathan stepped out onto the deck.

Nathan wore white slacks, a white silk shirt, a gorgeous navy blazer, and deck shoes with no socks.

Carly wore a white satin dress with navy blue

satin trim along the hem of the skirt and the square neckline.

They couldn't take their eyes off each other. At that moment I think they were the happiest two people in the world—unless, of course, you counted Ava and me.

❀

"Look! Here's one of you and Gina Gupta." I held up the photo.

Mary-Kate took it. "Wow! I'm definitely posting this on my Web site. Any more pictures with you or me in them?"

"Lots," I answered.

The wedding reception had lasted until 2:00 A.M. Mary-Kate and I had our pictures taken with tons of movie stars and celebrities. I had a great one of Nathan and me.

Carly and Nathan were on their honeymoon in Paris. Mary-Kate and I were at Ava's, putting together their wedding album. It was the last part of the job, and Mary-Kate was helping me.

"Here's one of you and Ava dancing," she said.

I looked at the photo and sighed. "I hope the next time I'm invited to a celebrity wedding, I'll have a date."

Mary-Kate pushed her hair back over her shoulders. "Just wait until school starts again. You'll have more dates than you can count."

"I hope you're right. But I do know this—they won't be with Aaron. Lauren called this morning and said she saw him with somebody else at the mall yesterday."

"Does that make you unhappy?" Mary-Kate asked.

"Not really. I think Aaron and I were perfect for each other for a while. But things change." I shrugged. There didn't seem to be any other explanation.

I still couldn't believe that anybody could be as fake as Greg Johnson was. Mary-Kate and I spent a lot of time trying to come up with a good idea for revenge.

In the end we figured, why bother? Mary-Kate pointed out that, based on Greg's information, *Celebrity View* printed a lot of stuff about Carly and Nathan's wedding that turned out to be wrong.

When the real photographs of the wedding had hit the newspapers, *Celebrity View* looked incredibly stupid. The paper lost gobs of credibility, and Greg Johnson would probably never get a job in journalism again.

I couldn't have asked for a more picture-perfect ending.

Mary-Kate and Ashley's

GRADUATION SUMMER

is about to begin!

Senior prom, graduation, saying good-bye to old friends and making new ones. For Mary-Kate and Ashley, this is the summer that will change their lives forever . . . *Graduation Summer*. And they can't wait!

NEW

Coming soon!
GRADUATION SUMMER
#1 We Can't Wait!
#2 Never Say Good-bye
#3 Everything I Want

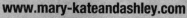

mary-kate olsen
ashley olsen
eugene levy
R
new york minute
In Theaters May 7th
www.newyorkminutemovie.com
WARNER BROS. PICTURES